"I w   e
said.   t
would be a lie."

…e swallowed hard. "Woul…

…es. I don't need the mone…
…as a boutique hotel. I d…
…uld come in from buying…
…' father to have it. And that's where you come in."

…e?"

…was a nice accident, seeing that your home was
…ut to be foreclosed on. I thought I might be able to
…p you out. For a fee."

…fee?"

…ere is no such thing as a free lunch. Or, in your
…e, a free manor home a reasonable commuter
…ance from the city."

…u must realize that I don't have anything to give
…," she said, her heart sinking into her stomach at
about the same moment the back of her neck started
…rickle. He must know she didn't have money.
Which meant he must want something else. And that
couldn't be anything good.

…ave a proposition for you."

…gave him a pointed glare and drew on every
…d of strength she'd been building in herself for
…past year. "If this has anything to do with filling
…position in your life that my mother filled in your
…ier's you can take your proposition and shove it up
…r—"

…'d like you to be my wife."

Maisey Yates was an avid Mills & Boon® Modern™ Romance reader before she began to write them. She still can't quite believe she's lucky enough to get to create her very own sexy alpha heroes and feisty heroines. Seeing her name on one of those lovely covers is a dream come true.

Maisey lives with her handsome, wonderful, diaper-changing husband and three small children across the street from her extremely supportive parents and the home she grew up in, in the wilds of Southern Oregon, USA. She enjoys the contrast of living in a place where you might wake up to find a bear on your back porch and then heading into the home office to write stories that take place in exotic urban locales.

Recent titles by the same author:

HAJAR'S HIDDEN LEGACY
THE ARGENTINE'S PRICE
THE HIGHEST PRICE TO PAY
MARRIAGE MADE ON PAPER

Did you know these are also available as eBooks?
Visit www.millsandboon.co.uk

GIRL ON A DIAMOND PEDESTAL

BY
MAISEY YATES

MILLS &
BOON

First published in Great Britain 2012
by Mills & Boon, an imprint of Harlequin (UK) Limited.
Harlequin (UK) Limited, Eton House, 18-24 Paradise Road,
Richmond, Surrey TW9 1SR

© Maisey Yates 2012

ISBN: 978 0 263 89052 5

Harlequin (UK) policy is to use papers that are natural, renewable and recyclable products and made from wood grown in sustainable forests. The logging and manufacturing process conform to the legal environmental regulations of the country of origin.

Printed and bound in Spain
by Blackprint CPI, Barcelona

GIRL ON A
DIAMOND PEDESTAL

To my mom, Peggy,
for always encouraging me to simply be me.

And many thanks to Robyn, Gabby, Nicola,
for giving me coaching on my Australian phrases.

CHAPTER ONE

BIRCH Manor was the last constant left. The only thing remaining in her life that had always been there. Everyone else, her mother, her piano teacher, her fans…they were gone. The house was all she had.

Until the bank took it, at least.

Noelle sighed and looked out the window, her stomach tightening as the glossy black Town Car drove through the open wrought-iron gates and around the circular drive, stopping in front of the door to the manor.

She moved away from the window and hoped her guest didn't notice the twitching curtains. It was too sad really, that she'd been reduced to this. Waiting for her home to be taken, watching for the financier coming to appraise the property. Waiting to be evicted. She had no idea where she would go.

The check she'd gotten last week had come with a handwritten note informing her that this would likely be the last royalty check for the foreseeable future. The company wasn't selling her old albums anymore, and several of her digital albums had been taken down from the big websites. No one wanted her music.

Not that the royalties had been amazing over the past year. Hardly anything really, enough to buy a latté on the odd occasion. Now she wouldn't even have that any more.

Suddenly she wanted the hot, frothy drink so badly she thought she might cry.

She was a sad case. Poor Noelle. She'd throw a pity party if she thought anyone would come. Well, the bank might if there was something to repossess. She laughed into the vast, empty entryway, then straightened her skirt and took her place in front of the door, not really sure why she was bothering to play hostess, only that it was reflexive. Her mother would have expected it of her. Demanded it.

Of course, her mother wasn't here.

Noelle sucked in a sharp breath and reached for the doorknob. Her fingers tightened around it, waiting for the knock, and as soon as it pierced the silence, she tugged the door open. Her heart skipped, spinning a downward spiral into her stomach as she took in the man standing before her.

Tall and broad, in a suit that was definitely not of the standard-issue, bank-employee variety, but quality, custom made and tailored to flatter his amazing, masculine physique.

His lips curved into a smile, not a warm one, but one that she felt down to her toes. His eyes were dark, deep like chocolate, but without any of the sweetness. Her stomach tightened, a strong, sharp craving overwhelming her.

For coffee. Still coffee.

"Ms. Birch?" He had a nice voice too, rich and luxuriant, just like the suit. Why couldn't it have been obnoxious? Nasal or high or something. But no, it was low and husky, smooth with a drop-dead-sexy Australian accent adding flavor to his words.

"Yes. Are you…" She changed tactics mid sentence, decided to go for something more forceful. "You're from the bank."

He stepped past her and into the house, his eyes sweeping the room, and her, in a dismissive manner. "Not exactly."

"Then why are you here?"

"I came in lieu of the assessor. I'm interesting in making an offer on the property."

"It's in foreclosure."

"I know. And I'm considering purchasing it before it goes to auction. I need to take a look and let the bank know what I intend to pay for it."

"Really? Why didn't I think of that? I would have given them…well, I think I might have five dollars in my bag over there." She gestured to the red purse hanging on its hook by the door. "Think they'd go for it?"

"Not likely." His answer was clipped, annoyed. Why was he annoyed? She hadn't barged into *his* home early on a Saturday morning. She was the one who got to be annoyed. It was her right.

"Too bad," she said, fighting to keep her tone light, flippant. Unaffected.

"From what I've seen of your loan information, you've been delinquent for months."

Delinquent. She hated that term. Like she was a criminal or something because she didn't have any money. Like she wouldn't have paid the mortgage if her bank balance ever managed to exceed double digits.

"I'm aware of why you're here—or, at least, I'm aware of what I did to make the bank take my house back." The words stuck in her throat. "I don't need a rundown from you."

"Good. Because I'm not here to give it."

"No. You're here to find out if you want to move into my home before the bank has even thrown me out onto the streets," she bit out. She never would have spoken to anyone that way a year ago. She would have been gracious, smiled, been faultless in every way. But that veneer had started eroding over the past year. She just felt angry now. Battered. Like she was dying slowly inside as life chipped away at her very last foothold.

She'd been trained never to show strain or fatigue, never, ever to give the tabloid media a reason to gossip about her. But the past year had been like hell on earth. A constant barrage of blows that never seemed to end. Every time she tried to stand up and dust herself off, something else would hit. And this seemed like the knock-out punch. Because what would she do without this last piece of security? Without this last link to everything she used to be?

Everything she would never be again.

"That's where you're wrong, Noelle," he said, his dark eyes locked with hers. She felt like he could see her—not just that he was looking at her, but that he truly saw *into* her, beneath her polished veneer to the cluttered mess beyond.

She wanted to hide. Not just from him, but from everything.

Isn't that what you've been doing for more than a year now?

Yes. Head down, trying to survive. Trying not to draw media attention. Too defeated to try and track her mother down. Because, as the lawyer she hadn't been able to afford had pointed out, the money had all been in her mother's name, so the battle would be long and expensive. It would devour the fortune that she was trying to win back. And if she didn't win…it would mean the kind of debt she could never crawl out of. It all seemed impossibly hopeless.

"Then do enlighten me, Mr…?"

"Grey." He extended his hand and she accepted the offer, his strong, masculine fingers curling around her slender, pale hand, engulfing it. Making her feel warm, too warm. "Ethan Grey."

Ethan felt a flash of attraction, of pure, raw need, race through him when his hand touched Noelle's soft skin. He ran through a litany of his very favorite swear words in his head. It had been too long since he'd gotten laid if a handshake had the power to get him hot.

Especially a handshake from this particular woman.

Maybe it's genetic?

He bit back a sound of disgust at that thought. He would never use that as an excuse. He was in control of his own actions. If he sinned, it was because he'd chosen it. And at least he was man enough to admit it. Unlike his father. Damien Grey hadn't been much of a role model in that respect.

Yes, she was beautiful, but mostly just fragile-looking with her delicate frame and pale skin. As if she didn't get outside enough. Everything about her was pale. White-blond hair, large, robin's-egg-blue eyes with long, thick lashes, darkened with the aid of makeup. She was like a porcelain doll, one that might break if handled too roughly.

The deep-red lipstick she was wearing was likely intended to give her more color, but all it did was show just how washed out the rest of her was. Pale and drawn, shadows beneath luminous blue eyes.

Even so, she was arresting. Her beauty was almost other-worldly.

She reminded him so much of her mother. That cold, self-possessed allure that made a man ache to see what was beneath all that control. The kind of woman who led men around on leashes, had them begging simply to be in her presence.

She had all of that, plus an air of vulnerability her mother hadn't had. It only added to her appeal. It made a man want to do more than simply possess. It made him want to protect.

"Nice to meet you," she mumbled, pulling her hand away.

He was relieved by the break in contact. "I don't think you really mean that."

She smiled, an expression that didn't reflect in her eyes. "No. You're right, but I'm too polite to say otherwise."

"I'm glad for your manners then," he said dryly.

"How is it I've misunderstood your motives, Mr. Grey?"

"I'm not planning on moving into your house."

She arched an eyebrow. "No?"

"No. I plan on expanding the house and making it a hotel property."

"What?"

She was small, maybe a foot shorter than his own height of six foot three. But there was nothing small about her presence. Even in her pale, diminished state she exuded a kind of force that demanded all eyes rest on her. Another similarity to her mother. At least from what he remembered of the woman. He'd been young the times he'd seen her, lingering near the gates to his childhood home, his father sneaking out to be with her like an adolescent boy. Leaving his wife and son behind so he could indulge in his forbidden passion.

Ethan clenched his hands into fists and forced his mind back to the present. He'd been over the past. Over and over it. Now was the time for action and he couldn't afford to be distracted. Not when the key to his plan was standing right in front of him.

"How can you do that?" she asked, not waiting for him to answer. "This house is two hundred years old. It's...it's a marvel of architecture and...and...it's my home." Her voice cracked on the last word.

He knew that this was the only home in her name. He wasn't sure what had happened to the penthouse in midtown Manhattan, or the townhouse in Paris. When the sprawling estate had come up as a home in foreclosure he'd acted immediately. It was opportunistic on his part, more than a carefully planned-out maneuver. But from the moment he'd walked in, he knew he'd made the right move.

Strange how largely she and her mother had factored into his life, while she seemed to have no clue who he was. He hadn't seen even a hint of recognition in her eyes, either on sight or at the sound of his name.

She was probably too dazzled by the brilliance of her own sparkle to look around and see anyone other than herself.

"I'm not planning on demolishing it, Noelle, merely expanding it. Adding a pool, maybe."

She flinched when he said that. It bothered her, him talking about changing the house. She was attached to it, that much was obvious. And that would prove useful to him.

"Great, well, I don't really want to be involved in the blueprint for this, so maybe I should leave and let you poke around for a while?"

"I don't believe I need to spend any time poking around. My mind is made up. It's a good investment and from where I'm standing it doesn't appear that I'll take a loss on it."

The expression in her eyes changed again. Anger, pure and real, joined the anguish. So much emotion in her. He couldn't summon up a single feeling in response. Too many years of shoving them aside. Of strangling the life out of his emotions whenever possible so he could move forward.

"So you can just buy it then? Like that? Without even

stopping to consider what it might do to your…to your monthly budget or anything like that?"

He laughed. It was only a sound. It didn't really express any of the things laughter usually did. "Not my main concern, no."

He could see the struggle in her, the emotions that made her body tremble even as she kept her face set into a firm, determined expression. She wasn't exactly what he'd imagined she might be. Pampered, yes. Clear prima donna tendencies, yes. But she was strong too. He was certain that beneath that brittle, fragile exterior was a backbone of steel. That only made her more interesting.

"Why is the house so important?" He was hoping it was important. Everything depended on it.

Because it all depended on her. On getting her to agree to his proposition. Revenge was sweet, but she would give it the bitter edge that he craved. That he needed in order to have satisfaction.

"*Why? Why do you think?*" she asked, her voice breaking again. "It's the only home I have. When the bank takes it, I won't get any money from the sale. I'll have nothing. Less than nothing. I have nowhere to go."

"Most single women don't live by themselves in a mansion that could easily house ten other families," he said.

Noelle fought to keep her cool, to keep from breaking down. From showing any weakness. She had been trained to look calm on the surface no matter what. If her mother tore into her before a show, telling her she wasn't beautiful anymore, that it was her fault ticket sales were down, she still had to go on stage. And she would keep every emotion locked in her, letting it escape through her fingertips. In the sound of the piano.

Her emotion didn't seem able to escape that way anymore. Now when she played it was dry, stilted. There was nothing behind it. Nothing but empty, technical skill.

She took a breath. "It's not a matter of downsizing, although that would have helped the electric bill." A bill she had done her very best to scale back. No lights during the day, no heat, the only source of warmth the fireplace in her bedroom so she didn't freeze at night. "I don't have anything," she said, shame creeping over her.

He arched one dark eyebrow, his expression cool, blank of any sort of caring or true interest. "How is that possible?"

The last thing she wanted to do was give him her big bad sob story. She'd found a lot of strength over the past year. Just getting up had been a struggle some days, but she'd done it. And she'd done it with no support. Asking for help now violated that sense of independence and pride. But she was staring homelessness in the face and she wasn't certain her pride came into it anymore.

"Everything's gone. Don't you know what happens to child stars when their parents manage everything? It's a story that gets repeated on entertainment news channels quite frequently."

She wasn't a child now, which was why she'd become so uninteresting to the public. Concert halls were half-empty when before she'd filled them. A nine-year-old girl playing original compositions on a massive grand piano was a spectacle. It was amazing. A woman doing the same thing lacked the wow factor.

Empty halls meant more pressure. More drills. More practice. Something was wrong and it was her fault. And then it had all stopped. The music quit playing in her head. She looked at a beautiful landscape, at people on the sidewalk, and she heard nothing. Once, it had all been enanced by the soundtrack in her mind. Melodies that came bout constantly, endlessly.

It was quiet now. Dead.

"They took everything," he said.

"My mother did." The betrayal was still like an open wound inside her, something she couldn't seem to reconcile or heal.

That got a slight reaction from him, a bit of real shock in his dark eyes. "And she's gotten away with it?"

"It's all in her name," she said. "Most of my money was earned before I turned eighteen and even after that I never bothered to change anything. I mean, why would I? She had always managed my finances and I trusted her. I have no contract saying any of it should have been mine, or that I earned it. So that's how I ended up with nothing." She paused for a moment and looked up at the ceiling. "Well, this house is in my name, so yay me."

The only person who knew about her mother was the lawyer she'd spoken to. She hadn't been able to bear the thought of telling anyone else. The fact that her own mother would do that to her. Her piano teacher had quit. Friends, people she'd toured with sometimes, were still busy making music. And she was alone.

In an old empty house with bills that she could never hope to pay. She'd been treading water until recently, working on a plan, some sort of solution…but now she was going under. And she knew she would drown before any sort of help came along.

Ethan knew he shouldn't really be shocked that Noelle's mother had betrayed her like that. A bitch like her didn't care who she hurt. She certainly hadn't cared about the pain she'd caused his mother. Not in the least.

But as much as he hated Noelle's mother for her part, it was his father Damien who had to pay for the sins of the past. And Noelle was in the perfect position to make that a reality.

He ignored the slight twinge of conscience he began to feel in his chest, spreading to his arms, making his fingertips feel numb. He didn't have time for a conscience. Noelle would get what she needed, and he would get exactly what he wanted.

Everyone would win.

Except for his father.

"Will you be touring again soon?" he asked.

Noelle had been touring since she was a child. He'd never been to see her, but he'd seen her name in the news frequently. She'd played at Carnegie Hall, she'd played for the Queen of England. She was a household name and had been for at least eleven years. And apparently, all of that touring had left her with nothing.

"I'm not touring anymore," she said tightly. "My label dropped me because I couldn't book venues. My publicist dropped me. My agent." She made a clicking sound with her tongue. "So, yeah, I'm pretty much done with music."

She looked down, lashes fanning over high cheekbones that seemed a bit more pronounced than they should be. She had that cabbage-soup-diet look about her, like she wasn't getting quite enough to eat. He couldn't imagine her turning down his proposition, not when he knew she needed it so badly.

And he was tempted, tempted to come out with it now.

But it was too soon.

He was a master of the business deal, and tomorrow, he would set in motion the most important deal of his life. He wouldn't allow impatience to ruin that.

"Come to my office tomorrow," he said. "I'll send a car for you around noon."

"Why? So we can discuss where in my hundred-year-old rose garden you're going to dig your inground pool?"

"Not exactly."

He had no intention of turning her home into a hotel. He had no intention of purchasing it at all. Sure, a hotel here would bring in money, but that money would be nothing compared to the satisfaction he would gain by executing vengeance against his father.

Noelle, and her home, were the key to that revenge.

CHAPTER TWO

ETHAN'S office building was warm. Noelle let it wash over her as she walked into the open, stately marble foyer and crossed to an elevator that took her to the top floor.

Even the elevator spoke of luxury. She ached for it. For gorgeous hotels with amazing views and thousand-thread-count sheets. For heat, and for lunch that consisted of more than instant noodles with little freeze-dried chunks of vegetables.

For a crowded auditorium and applause meant just for her.

"You really are pathetic," she said to the empty lift.

Yes, she really was. But knowing that didn't make the longing go away. Her life had never been easy, she knew that. Sometimes she'd wished for all of the fame, the practice, the shrill voice of her mother and the stern voice of her instructor to go away.

But now that they had, she was faced with some harsh realities she'd never dealt with before.

She sucked in a sharp breath as the elevator stopped. Her stomach turned over, her hands shook as if she was about to go out on stage. The kick of adrenaline was addictive. It was one of the many things she missed about her former life as a concert pianist.

This was different though. The familiar spike of adrenaline was infused with a warm, honeyed sensation that pooled in her stomach and made her body ache in places she'd never given a thought to.

She clenched her teeth and took a breath. *Focus.*

She walked from the lift to a reception area and gave her name to the man sitting behind the desk. While he searched for it in the computer, she picked one of her favorite pieces—not one of her own, but one of Mozart's—and began to run through the notes.

Pictured her fingers flying over the keys. Effortlessly, joyfully.

It was something she always did before a performance, to remind her of how prepared she was. That she was ready. That she wouldn't make a mistake.

"Just through that door there, Ms. Birch," the receptionist said, smiling brightly.

"Thank you," she replied, keeping her mind on the music as she walked to the door.

She tried to slow her breathing, keeping it in rhythm with the legato portion of the piece. *Slow and steady. Don't rush. Don't falter. Smooth.*

She opened the door and the notes fluttered from her head like startled birds. She wasn't prepared for whatever this meeting was, and there was no use pretending otherwise.

Because Ethan was more frightening than a theater filled with three thousand people. He was sitting behind a broad, neat desk, his large hands folded in front of him, his expression even harder than it had been yesterday at her house.

"Good morning," he said, unfolding his hands and putting them behind his head, the action so casual it was maddening. That he wasn't tense at all when she felt like a slight breeze could shatter her was beyond unfair.

"Morning," she said, refusing to lie and call it good. "I'm here for our mysterious meeting."

"Have a seat," he offered, gesturing to the chair in front of his desk.

"No." She wasn't going to put herself in that position. Him behind his big desk, her sitting there on the opposite side like a child about to be scolded.

Being meek and subservient didn't work. It didn't keep people with you. It only made you easier to deal with. And this past year she'd come to see that she'd been being thoroughly dealt with all of her life. That was one good result of having a bomb detonated in the middle of her existence. She wasn't going to play the pawn anymore.

A harsh lesson learned the hard way. But she *had* learned it. In some ways, without her gilded cage, she was stronger now than she'd ever been. Even if it didn't always feel like it.

A half smile curved his lips. She didn't like that. Because it wasn't an amused smile, it was something else. Something sort of dark beneath the surface of the expression. "No?"

"I'd prefer to stand," she said stiffly.

He inclined his head. "If you like."

He stood then, and she felt dwarfed. He was a foot taller than she was, and broad. More than that, he just seemed to fill the room with his presence. The something else that gave people whiplash as they passed him in the street, trying to get a look at him. Mad sex appeal or something. She stretched her neck and straightened her shoulders. It didn't help.

"I would say that this was business," he said. "That it's not personal. But that would be a lie."

She swallowed hard. "Would it?"

"Yes. I don't need the money your home would bring

in as a boutique hotel. I don't need the money that would come in from buying the family business, Grey's. But I don't want him to have it. And that's where you come in."

"Me?"

"It was a nice accident, seeing that your home was about to be foreclosed on. I thought I might be able to help you out. For a fee."

"A fee?"

"There is no such thing as a free lunch. Or, in your case, a free manor house situated a reasonable commuter distance from the city."

"You must realize that I don't have anything to give you," she said, her heart sinking into her stomach at the same moment that the back of her neck started to prickle. He must know she didn't have money. Which meant he must want something else. And that couldn't be anything good.

"You've never heard my name?" he asked.

"No," she said. "Should I have heard it?"

"I know yours. And not just because you're famous. Or, more accurately, I know your mother's name."

"How?"

"Do you know the name Damien Grey?"

"I…" She almost said no. But it was a name she knew, not the last name, but the first. A very familiar name. "Yes. Well, Damien, but…it could be a different Damien."

"I'm betting not. Damien Grey is my father, and for several years, he was your mother's lover."

As revelations went, it shouldn't have been shocking. It wasn't as though she'd believed her mother had been out having tea parties while Noelle spent nights alone in grand hotel suites before performances, but her mind had never gone there.

She did remember her mother talking about Damien,

though. Meeting him. Staying with him. She'd been eight, maybe, when that had started and she simply hadn't put the relationship in the right context.

"I always thought he was in the music industry," she said, realizing how stupid that sounded. She shook her head. "But what does this have to do with me? Or is it all part of drawing out the torture that has been the past year of my life? I'm not quite dead yet, want to land the fatal blow?"

"I have a proposition for you."

She gave him a pointed glare and drew on every shred of strength she'd been building in herself for the past year. "If this has anything to do with filling the position in your life that my mother filled in your father's, you can take your proposition and shove it up your—"

"I'd like you to be my wife."

She took a step back and sucked in air, choking on it, coughing and coughing while trying to catch her breath.

"Are you all right?" Ethan took a step toward her and she held up her hand, gesturing for him to stop. A gesture he ignored.

He put his hand on her back, his touch warm and…comforting, in some strange way. A connection. She hadn't had a connection with anyone in so long. She wondered if she ever truly had.

She cleared her throat and breathed deeply. "I'm fine now." She stepped away from him.

"Do you need something?"

She'd have to make a list.

Yesterday's craving came back to her in full force. "A latte?"

He nodded and walked back to his desk, pressing the intercom button on his phone. "Christophe, I need a latte." He looked back at Noelle. "How do you like it?"

"Vanilla. With whipped cream."

He repeated the instructions to Christophe then cut off the connection.

"It will be here soon," he said.

She wanted to cry, and it was the stupidest thing. Yet she couldn't stop the ache of emotion that tightened her throat. No, it wasn't emotion, she told herself. It was her recent choking experience. That was all. "Thank you."

"Now, shall I repeat my offer or will it send you into a fit again?"

She narrowed her eyes. "I choked. Although if it had been a fit, it wouldn't be overly surprising, would it?"

"Marriage in exchange for your home. Free and clear, not owned by the bank, but by you."

Well, wasn't that a bright shiny poison apple? *Take a bite, dearie.* "What's the catch? Why me?"

"I thought you might have a bigger stake in this than a stranger would. Think about your mother seeing you in the news, rising back to the top on my arm. The simple truth is, I need a wife to get the company. And if that wife was you, if you were a part of taking it from my father's grasping hands, well, it would be that much sweeter."

"That's...I don't know. I don't know if I can be involved in this. It's..."

"Let me simplify it. If you marry me, in name only, and divorce me once Grey's is transferred into my name, you get your house. And the rest of it doesn't need to matter to you."

"How can it not matter to me?" she asked.

He shrugged. "That's up to you. But how do you think it would be for your mother to see you in the paper, to see you back at the top? In circles she can't move in any more, not once you're in them. Because then they might find out what she did to you. Maybe you don't have legal recourse, but you can close her out of society. If I remember her correctly, that mattered a great deal to her."

Noelle tried to think through the pulse pounding in her temple. "Yes. It did. Does."

"Wouldn't it be nice to take a piece of that back from her?"

Yes. Yes it would. And no, she didn't think she was bigger than that. Because all her life, she'd been nothing more than her mother's ticket in. A chance for her to move in the circles she'd always dreamed of while Noelle did all the work to keep her there.

"How do I know I can trust you?" she asked.

"How do you know you can trust anyone?"

Noelle thought of her mother. Of finding out one day that the penthouse in Manhattan was empty…and so was her bank account. "I suppose you can't."

"Time. A blood relationship. Marriage vows. None of it can ensure you know someone. But you have nothing to lose. You can only gain. You don't have anything else for me to take."

Well, that wasn't entirely true, but she wasn't planning on announcing it anytime soon. "But this would be…" She fought the blush creeping into her face. "Not a real marriage, right?"

"A real wedding. A legal marriage. But nothing more. Nothing permanent or physical."

"Oh." It sounded simple. Uncomplicated and…tempting. A chance not only to get her home back, but to have the bank stop calling and sending notices. A chance to show her mother she hadn't won.

"In the interest of us knowing each other better, I'm going to ask you some questions and you will answer me. Honestly."

Noelle blinked, the change of topic making her head spin. "Are you interviewing me for the position?"

"As any good businessman would."

Noelle shifted, uncomfortable beneath his assessing gaze.

"I know you've never been married," he said.

"No." She shook her head.

"Do you have a man in your life? A lover?"

She nearly laughed. Where would she have kept a lover? In her suitcase while they were on the road? Her mother would never have allowed such a thing. Sure, *she* got to make time for men, but she would never have permitted Noelle the same luxury. Would never have let her compromise her image like that. And now… Well, she wasn't about to bring a date back to her big empty house and tell him all about how washed-up she was over a cup of bargain-brand soda.

"Not at the moment," she replied dryly.

"Good. It would have to remain that way for the duration of the arrangement. For appearances."

"I think I can manage that."

An answering smile curved his lips. "Excellent."

"And I'll get my house?"

"And then some."

"What else?" she asked, hating that she cared. Hating that she was tempted.

"I would give you a settlement when we divorced. That's in addition to all the media attention you'll get as a result of our association. I attend a lot of events and as my fiancée, you would attend with me."

The longing that assaulted her was like a great, dark pit opening up inside. Empty and huge, waiting to be filled. Needing it.

Parties and people and cameras. Luxury. Things that

had been so absent from her life. A link to the girl she'd been, the things she'd had. This was a chance to have it again. She despised the weakness in her that wanted it. That needed it.

And yet she felt crushed by the desire for it.

There was a quiet knock on the door and Christophe came in, latte in hand. The wide-mouthed caramel-colored mug was like a vessel of life in her eyes. She hadn't bought coffee in weeks, months maybe. Not even for the machine at home.

She took it in her hands and let the heat from the ceramic seep into her palms. "Thank you," she murmured, her throat tight again.

Christophe smiled and made a hasty exit, as she imagined he was paid to do. Quiet efficiency.

She took a sip and was horrified when her eyes blurred with tears. She blinked hard as she swallowed the warm, comforting liquid, allowing it to soothe the pain in her chest.

She lowered the cup and looked fixedly at the swirl of thick cream on the top of her latte.

A flash of recognition mingled with the image of a headline in her mind. *He's offering you this. A way to escape. A way out.*

And a way to prove to your mother that she didn't win.

"So this would be a marriage as far as legalities go, but not…not permanent and not physical," she repeated.

"Exactly. No one, including my father, needs to know the personal aspects of the relationship. But it is imperative we make it down the aisle. I came close once, and it's going to take more than close to get what I want."

She nodded. Tried to picture it. Tried to picture getting married. Funny how she'd never really thought about it before. She'd played at weddings, celebrity weddings, weddings for royalty, but she'd never once thought of her own.

Her scope had always been so narrow. She'd lived and breathed piano. Performance, composition, practice, drills…she had dreamed music. It had been her all-consuming passion and drive. And when it had faltered, her mother had always been there to push her past it. To make sure that she didn't lose focus for even a moment.

It was good in a way. She didn't have a romantic fantasy tied to the thought of wedding. A wedding was…well, it was paper. Paper with performance added into the mix. And she did performance. At least she had done it. She'd done it well, too.

A kind of restless energy overtook her, starting in her fingertips, tingling up her arms and to her stomach. Why not do it? How was it really different than any other performance she'd given? She'd always projected a character on stage. Serene and sweet no matter what was going on inside of her. No matter if she'd been fighting with her mother or if she'd suffered a slap across the face at the other woman's hands ten minutes before show time. She just added another layer of powder and went out on stage, smile pasted on.

"It's a temporary arrangement. A business proposition. And I would pay you well."

"And we would be expected to…go out. Go to parties, that sort of thing." It shamed her that it mattered, almost more than the money. To be bathed in the glow of admiration again. Nothing felt like that. Nothing. It made her feel that she was a part of something, that she was important. That she was loved.

And she'd been so alone for so long. Hiding, hoping no one would find out what had happened.

"Yes. We would have to at least give the appearance of a courtship, even if it is a whirlwind one."

"Stranger things have happened, I suppose."

"Much stranger."

"Like a mother making off with her daughter's earnings?"

He nodded. "Or a father betraying his family to spend time with his mistress."

And this was a chance, for both of them, to make some of it right. And maybe she was making it more than it was because right now the latte was so warm and so comforting, and the caffeine was making her feel more awake and alive than she had in weeks but it seemed slightly poetic in nature.

They had both been manipulated. Betrayed in a way. They had both lost things they had earned, things that were theirs by right, at the hands of those who were supposed to love them.

They deserved to take those things back. They both deserved to win.

"You'll put this all in a...a contract, right?" She had learned the hard way that even her own mother couldn't be trusted, she wasn't about to put her trust in a man she'd only just met.

"We'll have a prenup. Of course it won't outline the specifics of the arrangement, as we don't want that made public. The house will be yours upon the signing of our marriage license, money after the divorce."

"You've thought this through."

A wicked grin curved his lips. "I'm making it up as I go along, but I've been told I'm pretty good at improvising."

"I would say so."

She wasn't. She was pretty crap at improvising, as it happened. The whole last year was proof of that.

"I've begun the paperwork with the bank to purchase the manor. I'll sign it over to you once we speak the vows."

"And the prenup?"

"My lawyer can have it ready by tomorrow."

She felt dizzy. Her life had been stagnant for so long, nothing to mark the passing of months but a new mortgage bill in the mail. Now suddenly things were changing. She felt like she might be able to see the light at the end of the tunnel.

And there had been nothing but damp, dank cold for so long.

"Good," she heard herself say. She felt as if she were hovering above the scene now, watching it all with a surreal kind of detachment.

It didn't seem real, that was for sure. But it felt hopeful in a really strange way.

That marriage to a man she didn't know or love seemed hopeful said a lot about the sad state of her affairs, that was for certain.

"I'll see you tomorrow then," he said.

"Your place or mine?" she asked, trying to force a laugh.

A dark light shone in his eyes. "I'd say yours, since it is the thing that brought us together."

CHAPTER THREE

ETHAN could hear the music as soon as he walked up to the door of the manor. It wasn't a classical piece. It wasn't a song at all. Repetition and scales, the same few notes over and over again with regimented perfection. A straight, staccato rhythm more like a military maneuver than anything related to music.

Strange. He hadn't associated that kind of discipline with her. But then, she looked so much like her mother it was hard for him not to think of their personalities being as identical as their features. Celine Birch was a cloud of perfume and gauzy clothing in his memory. Frothy and elegant, nice even. It had taken some time to realize what she was.

His father's mistress. No, more than that. The woman Damien Grey had loved above his family. The woman he hadn't even bothered to hide from his wife.

Ethan gritted his teeth and raised his hand, pounding on the door hard and fast. The strains of the piano continued, unbroken, unyielding. He turned the knob and the door opened. He followed the sounds of the piano, his footsteps echoing as he crossed the marble tiled entryway and walked into the formal sitting room.

There were no interior lights on, the opulent crystal chandelier hanging from the ceiling was dark. The only illumination came from the sun shining through two large windows.

And then there was Noelle, sitting at the piano, her eyes fixed on a point in front of her rather than down at her fingers, playing the notes over and over again. The sun was like golden fire in her hair, illuminating it, giving the impression of a halo. He wondered how it was possible for someone who looked so angelic to set fire to a man's blood without so much as a sultry glance.

She looked up and the music stopped abruptly, her too-large eyes overly wide in her face. "Ethan." She scrambled around to the other side of the glossy white grand piano.

"Am I early?" He knew he wasn't.

"I…" She looked around for as if searching for something. "I don't have a clock in here."

"What are you working on?"

She shook her head and tucked a strand of glossy hair behind her ear. "Nothing. Drills. Keeping up my dexterity."

"Do you practice every day?"

"Yes."

"I didn't think you were doing music anymore."

She shrugged. "I don't have anything else to do."

He walked over to the piano and ran his fingers over the sleek body. "I don't have a piano in my penthouse."

She frowned slightly. "Do you play?"

He chuckled. "No."

"Then why…" she trailed off, her mouth falling open. "Oh."

"You didn't imagine you would continue to live out here in the country did you? Especially not after we're married."

"I hadn't really…I hadn't really thought about it."

"I'll be installing you in a penthouse suite in one of my

hotels. All the better to garner the proper attention and establish ourselves as a real couple."

She winced over his choice of words. "Right."

"Is that a problem?"

She shook her head. "I'm used to moving around." Actually, the habit of moving around was so ingrained in her that staying in one place for so long had actually felt wrong in many ways. This past year, stuck out in the weeds all by herself, had been more surreal than a different city every night.

"I trust you'll find everything to your satisfaction."

Although the idea of running into her seemed extremely appealing.

"Great." She bit her lip and looked back at the piano.

"Do you need it in Manhattan?"

"I don't…it's a pain to move pianos. Hardly worth it."

"I'll buy you a new one and have it moved into the suite."

He said it so casually, like the purchase of a piano that would run him six figures meant absolutely nothing. There was a time when it had been the same for her. She'd had an allowance, provided by her mother, with the money from touring, merchandise and album sales, and she'd wanted for nothing.

There had been so much money then. Money she'd earned. Money that had somehow never been hers.

"I can't ask you to do that."

"It's nothing, Noelle. As you mentioned before, I have no shortage of resources at my disposal. You and I are working together and I see no reason why this partnership can't be beneficial for the both of us."

She frowned slightly. "I suppose."

Noelle wasn't certain what to do with such an accommodating offer. That he cared about her need to play the piano seemed strange. Her playing didn't benefit him. Now, her mother had always made certain there was a piano in every hotel suite they used. She couldn't skip practice, not for one afternoon. Being on tour was no excuse. She always got her hours in on the piano. It was her job, and she worked at it as faithfully as anyone who went to an office every day.

Or well beyond that point. It was her only input into the business that was her career. Her mother did the networking. She went to the parties, talked to booking agents, labels and made sure all the needs per her tour rider were in order. It was all about making sure that Noelle Birch—the business—was in order. It was never about her as a person.

But Ethan just seemed to be concerned with what she wanted, what might make her happy. It was strange. It made her feel warm inside, more even than yesterday's latte. She liked that even less than his wicked smiles. Because she knew better than to trust those feelings. Than to trust people who acted like they cared.

"Do you have the prenup?" she asked, stomach suddenly filled with a shivering sensation.

"Yes." He reached into his interior suit-jacket pocket and took out a folded stack of papers.

His fingers brushed against hers as he passed them to her. He was warm, like his office. She unfolded the papers and skimmed them, her heart accelerating when she got to the part about children and custody.

"But we don't need…"

"This is mostly a standard document. As far as even my lawyer is concerned this is a real marriage. My grandfather wanted me to have stability. The kind I lacked growing up, I think. Of course, I'm of the opinion that marriage doesn't necessarily bring that sort of stability. You can understand why."

"Haven't you tried just explaining to him?"

"You don't explain things to my grandfather. There's no point. He knows everything already. He's coming from a good place. And I don't mind following his rules—if only because I have such an easy time bending them," he grinned.

She kept on reading the prenup, her eyes widening when she saw the settlement she was entitled to in the event of a divorce. An event that they already had planned.

"Enough?" he asked.

She cleared her throat. "I...yes."

It was generous. Not enough that she'd never have to work again, but enough to keep her out of abject poverty, and with the full ownership of the manor in addition to the cash settlement it was all more than enough.

She could sell the manor, get a smaller apartment in town. She'd have enough to buy lattes and eat more than a cup of instant noodles for dinner.

It was enough that she couldn't say no. Even if the whole situation made her want to get in the shower and scrub her skin until she could wash away the film it had left on her. Her mother sleeping with his father, hurting his family that way. The idea of marrying just so she could keep her house...

Okay, so it might seem mercenary marrying for money, but it wasn't a real marriage. And why shouldn't she be a little bit mercenary? Everyone in her life had looked out for themselves, they'd used her to make their position in life better. What was wrong with her doing something for herself? And she wasn't using Ethan, she was helping him. They were helping each other. It was a very good rationalization, anyway.

"Once we leave here, you aren't backing out."

She shook her head. "I won't. I can't."

"Just remember, you stand to lose a lot more than I do."

"There's no way I could forget that." She bit her lip hard, trying to block out the feeling of hopelessness that was rising up in her, a feeling she had become far too familiar with. "Do you have a pen?" she asked, holding out her hand and hoping he didn't notice the slight tremble in her fingers.

"You don't have to sign it yet. We haven't even applied for the license. The actual wedding won't be for a while. We'll have to establish ourselves as a couple. For my grandfather's satisfaction."

"But I'm ready to sign." She was ready to move forward. Ready to commit one hundred percent.

"Good." He took the documents from her and put them back in his pocket. "Are you ready to come with me now?"

"Now?"

"Why wait?"

She looked around the living room, at the last connection to her former life. "No reason. It might take me a while to pack."

"I can wait."

It was the kind of opulence that felt like both a half-remembered dream and her due at the same time. The kind she had almost forgotten about, but longed for. She'd been reminded, with full and brutal force, just how much she missed it yesterday in Ethan's office, the warmth and glamour surrounding her like a comforting blanket.

And now, in the open, expansive suite, she just wanted to throw Ethan out the door and turn circles like the little girl she'd never truly been.

"Does it meet your standards?" he asked, resting his broad, dark hand on the white marble bar top.

She turned and forced a smile, trying to ignore the growing ball of emotion in her chest. "Perfectly."

"I can have a piano brought in tomorrow, does that work for you?"

"Yes, absolutely." A piano too. To go with the lush, amazing view of Central Park. And money. All fine and good to stand on principle and pretend it didn't matter… when you had some. But when you didn't…well, that was when you realized how important money was. It might not buy happiness, but it paid power bills, bought food and clothes. Those things made her pretty happy.

The knot inside her grew larger, made it hard to breathe. She felt…the whole thing just felt wrong, and yet she didn't think she could walk away. It wasn't like she was sleeping with him. That would make it all truly reprehensible.

But she still felt as if she was selling herself.

Haven't you always sold yourself?

What else was performance anyway? She had always been the product. It wasn't just her music. If her music had been all people wanted from her, it wouldn't have mattered that she was an adult now. That she was no longer a cute little cherub dwarfed by the grand piano she played.

This was just a different venue.

And she wasn't going to sleep with him.

Her body felt hot all over just thinking about it. She had zero experience when it came to men, and while in theory she knew about sex—all about it, since she had a pretty curious nature and she'd done a lot of…reading on the subject—she'd never had a chance to put her knowledge into practice. When would she have found the time? And her mother would have…

She closed that thought off. She didn't care anymore. She had once—she had cared so much. She'd wanted to please her mother, her instructor, her fans and her tutor more than anything in the world. To earn love by being talented and easy to deal with, to give and give.

She had nothing to show for it.

She didn't care what her mother would think of her now. And, considering her mother's personal life, it would be hypocritical for her even to have an opinion. So she could sleep with Ethan if she wanted to. She didn't have to hide away, she didn't have to do drills every day and she didn't have to stay away from men.

A little tremor wracked her body. Sensual and shameful. Sensual because…well, Ethan just took her thoughts down that path. Shameful because, while in normal circumstances the idea might appeal, she wasn't out to sell her body in the interest of spiting her mother. No, things weren't as desperate as all that.

There was a quiet knock on the door and Ethan crossed behind her. She turned quickly. She wanted to make sure she could see him.

He opened the door without checking to verify who it was. "Yes?"

"Mr. Grey." An employee of the hotel, identified only by his highly polished name tag——his sharply tailored suit was as far from a hotel uniform as anything Noelle had ever seen——stood in the entryway. "When I heard you were here, I thought I would come and make sure that everything was—"

"Everything's fine, Thomas," Ethan said, moving to where Noelle was standing, his stance possessive. A clear sign that he was linking the two of them, proving to the employee just where things stood.

Of course, it was all for show. But he was as good as putting on a show as she had once been.

"Noelle will be staying here for the foreseeable future. Everything is to go to my account. Food and service, anything she wants."

She didn't—couldn't—believe that Ethan was truly giving her carte blanche to have whatever she wanted. All part of the show, she reminded herself. Because a man could hardly seem stingy in regards to his…whatever the world was meant to see her as at the moment.

A potential wife. A high-priced call girl.

Her heart thudded dully in her chest. They could see her as either, it wouldn't matter. Ethan would marry her in the end and that would put a bit of salve on her reputation. Of course, the reputation would blister again after the divorce, but that was the least of her worries. At the moment she had no reputation. Her star had fizzled out.

Ethan moved nearer to her, curling his arm around her waist, drawing her to his body. His fingers moved, idly, slowly, the touch feather light over her clothing. Yet it seemed to blaze a trail of fire that penetrated the thin fabric of her blouse, leaving smoldering embers in its wake that retained the heat long after the flame had moved on.

She tried to suppress the small shiver that raced up her spine, but she couldn't. Too much of her energy was focused on keeping her face neutral, keeping from conveying to Thomas that having a man's fingertips drifting over the line of her waist was anything more than a common occurrence.

"Yes, sir." Thomas nodded. "And will you be staying here as well? In the interest of providing you with the best service."

Yeah, right. More like in the interest of being nosy.

Ethan's fingers drifted further up her body, to her ribs, curling around, barely brushing the underside of her breast. She stiffened, not allowing the gasp that had climbed into her throat to escape, not allowing her face to betray her shock.

"I'll call down in the morning for room service when I'm here. Rest assured, I'll be certain my needs are met while I'm staying."

Her face was hot, it felt like the blood beneath it was boiling, pulsing as it rushed through her veins and lit her skin like a beacon. She sucked in a breath. "Or I will." There. This was a game. That's all it was. And she wasn't about to be bested.

She didn't need heaps of—or any—sexual experience in order to play the part.

Ethan caught her chin between his thumb and forefinger and tilted her face up so that she had to meet his liquid black gaze. "I have no doubt about that. In fact, I have a feeling I'll be requiring very little in the way of hotel room service."

Her pulse was pounding in her temples now, but she ignored it. Instead of shrinking away from him, as her body was screaming at her to do, she curled herself into him, putting her palm flat on his chest.

It was solid, well-muscled. She could feel the definition of his body beneath the layers of his crisp dress shirt and suit jacket. He didn't have the body of a man who spent all his time behind a desk.

He had the body of a man who worked out. Shirtless. Maybe he swam? Water sluicing over all that enticing, golden skin, muscles shifting and bunching, tensing and relaxing as he moved...

She chastised her imagination big-time for that unnecessary foray into fantasy.

Understandably, their little sex farce brought sex to mind, but that didn't mean she was allowed to indulge in thoughts like that.

No, she was allowed to. If she wanted to. Which she didn't. Because this thing with Ethan was a business transaction. And that meant sex and fantasy had no place in it. She had to remember that.

She pressed her palm more firmly against him, proving to herself that he was just a man. A person. A body. Nothing to get excited about. "I'll make sure you have whatever you need," she said, fighting to keep the tremor out of her voice.

Thomas, the nosy employee, forced a smile. "Excellent, sir, then if everything is to your liking…?"

"Yes, we're fine for now."

"I'll leave you then."

When he turned and left, Noelle let out a gust of breath and tried to extricate herself from Ethan's hold without flailing.

"I think the show is over," she said, gritting her teeth when he continued to hold onto her.

"Is it?" he released her. "Too bad. I enjoyed that very much."

"It was beyond thrilling," she said, her smile false, very purposefully false so he would know just how fake the sentiment was. She had a feeling he wasn't being sincere. Just trying to see if he could agitate her.

"You surprise me sometimes."

"Do I?" she asked, her teeth locked tightly together.

"The day we met you seemed very…pale."

"I was about to lose my home, and you were scoping out and making changes before my rear end had even h the gutter."

"True enough."

Pale. What a strange way to describe her. Or maybe no *Pale* sounded weak, washed-out. As if something had mor potential and yet wasn't reaching it. Her stomach sank a bit. That was her. She couldn't even argue.

She was beginning to find that lost potential now though. She just had to get her life back on track. Get some resources so that she had a square one to start from. Maybe she could play again. Maybe the music would come back to her. If she played this opportunity right, she would have a chance.

Without it, she would lose the only asset she possessed. She would be on her own again, with nothing. No job experience, and not a whole lot of real-life experience.

"A year ago I never would have had the courage to do this," she said. "But, way back then, I didn't recognize a very important truth."

"What's that, beautiful?"

Her stomach tightened when he said that. *Beautiful.* She used to feel beautiful sometimes. She wanted to feel beautiful again.

It's up to you to feel beautiful though. Everyone else could just be lying.

Yes, it was up to her.

"I learned that you can't count on anyone. The only person I can trust to hold my best interests in high regard is me. If I want to change things, I have to do it, because no one else will do it for me."

"A hard lesson to learn, but an important one," he said.

"Very. So I'm taking care of me. Of my best interests."

"Don't forget my best interests. Don't forget your end of the deal."

"I won't."

"Good." He leaned in, his scent teasing her sense. The only man she'd had any exposure to was her piano teacher, and he had smelled of hair grease and heavy cologne. Ethan smelled like soap, clean skin and a little bit of something unique that was simply…him. A smell that made her want to lean in to him, to lean on his strength.

No. The only strength she could trust was her own.

Of course, it would be better if she could find a decent amount of strength.

She swallowed heavily and took a step back. He took a step toward her and she stopped, rooted to the spot on the plush carpet.

"I'm glad you're intent on playing your part, Noelle. Because tonight," he lifted his hand and skimmed her cheek with his thumb, brushing a lock of her pale gold hair from her shoulder, "I'm going to show the world that you're mine."

CHAPTER FOUR

I'm not yours. I'm not anyone's.

Her words echoed in her head as she contorted her arm in order to pull the zipper up on the tiny black cocktail dress that Ethan had had sent to her room an hour earlier.

Her words were feeble because hey, power, he had it. But she didn't belong to him. That was how her mother had seen her, too. A thing she could own. A thing she could sell. It was a good thing she'd had musical abilities or there was no telling what her mother would have used her for.

She shuddered and bent over, lifting a foot up and tugging on one of the glittering, beaded high heels, also provided by Ethan. Or Ethan's personal shopper or assistant. He didn't exactly seem the type to go and pick up a pair of gorgeous, sparkly shoes.

She bent and started pulling on the other shoe, lost her balance and wobbled sideways, catching herself on the couch but still tumbling to the floor. She let a curse slip through her lips and then laughed.

"Not quite ready yet?"

She turned sharply at the sound of that rich, oh-so-sexy voice. "You didn't knock. Did you knock?"

"It's my hotel," he said, shrugging broad shoulders and walking over to the bar. From her vantage point on the ground he looked even taller, and slightly more infuriating than normal since he'd just caught her at a disadvantage.

"It's my room," she said.

A half grin tugged at the corner of his mouth. "I'm paying for it." He picked up a bottle of Scotch and poured himself just enough to fill the bottom portion of the glass. "Drink?"

"Soda?" she asked.

He raised his eyebrows. "Soda?"

"I have a one-drink limit if I'm going out in public. My mother's rule, but in cases like this, I've always found it to be a good one."

"Have you?" he opened the fridge that was set into the bar and produced a little glass bottle of lemon-lime soda.

"I've seen too many starlets sprawled out on the floor at a big party after too much heavy drinking."

He looked down at her, his lips curving upward. "Sprawled on the floor, eh?"

She pushed her shoe on the rest of the way and pulled herself up, tugging the hem of her dress down. "A clumsy moment isn't the same as getting completely drunk and making an ass out of yourself in public."

"Relax. Have a soda, it'll calm your nerves. Well, it won't, but here you go." He picked up the bottle and walked over to her, putting the cool glass in her hand.

She was surprised that it still felt cold. After being in his hand she'd half expected it to be hot. From him, his skin. And good grief, but he was handsome.

Rugged and polished at the same time, totally put together while maintaining a slightly dangerous edge. It was the glimmer in his brown eyes, the sort of devilish look that told a woman he knew how to be bad at just the right moments....

And here she was turning Ethan Grey into some kind

of simplistic fantasy. She was too innocent when it came to men and she knew it. It was too easy to imagine she could handle him when she knew nothing could be further from the truth. When it came to sexual games, she couldn't compete with him.

But at least she'd be comfortable at the party. At least there she'd be in her element. More than she'd been since her world had crashed, burned and crumbled at her feet.

"Thank you," she said, suddenly feeling very thirsty. As if she'd swallowed sawdust.

Ethan pushed his dark hair off his forehead, leaving it disheveled. Her fingers itched to put it back in place. She gripped the bottle tighter.

"Just about ready then?" he asked.

"Um... Yes. Ready."

If she just thought about the party, and not how it would feel to run her fingers through Ethan's hair, she just might make it through the night.

Ethan watched Noelle's eyes as they entered the grand ballroom, all decked out for the kind of pretentious party he didn't care a fig about. Her eyes were lit up, like everything else in the room. It was the brightest he'd seen her since the day he'd first met her, pale and drained in the foyer of her home.

This was the sort of party his mother had lived for. He remembered her looking the same way, getting ready to go somewhere, getting out of the house. It was the only thing that had made her smile. When she could go to an event and shine. When she could bask in the glow of her dimming fame and receive some form of adoration. The adoration he'd given her had never seemed to matter.

And his father...he had been too consumed with chasing after another woman. Lavishing his affection on her.

Making an ass of himself and embarrassing all of them because he couldn't control his libido. He'd never seen how being easy was supposed to make a man more virile, more of a man. In his estimation, control counted for a lot more.

And Damien Grey had never possessed any sort of control when it came to women. But Ethan was different. When it came to relationships, he was in charge. It began and ended when he wanted it to, and if he didn't have the time to invest in a relationship, he simply didn't.

Of course, now he was paying for the long bout of celibacy.

"Like it?" he asked, his throat tight.

Her arm was draped through his, her hips brushing against his as she walked. Every stroke of her soft curves was like getting licked by a flame. He had thought her insipid that first day…but tonight he was seeing the real woman.

She was beautiful, perfectly made-up with her blond hair pinned into a low bun and the fitted black dress skimming her curves. He'd just about swallowed his tongue walking into the room and seeing her sprawled on the floor, long shapely legs exposed up to the tops of creamy, toned thighs.

He couldn't remember the last time the sight of a woman's legs had gotten him so hot.

Disgust rolled through him. Was he really letting her get to him so easily? Just because she had feminine curves and a hot pair of legs? She was also the daughter of the woman who had torn his life apart. There should be no attraction there. He should look at her and see Celine Birch. And yet he didn't.

Attraction or not, he wouldn't act on it. He wasn't his

father. He thought with the brain in his head, not the one in his pants.

"It's lovely. Amazing. Whose party is it?"

He realized he hadn't told her. He used that much-needed distraction to get his body back under control. "Birthday party. One of the big important socialite types."

"Which one?"

"Sylvie Ames."

"Oh, I played at one of Sylvie's birthdays. Her sweet sixteen. I remember it." Her cheeks flushed pink and she seemed to shrink a little bit beside him.

"When was that?"

"More than ten years ago."

"How old were you?" She seemed too young to have been doing anything on a grand scale ten years ago. Or even three years ago.

"I was eleven." She *had* been too young. He'd known she'd been a famous child, had even had a vague concept of who she was when his father had been sleeping with Celine, her mother. But it hadn't really struck him until that moment just how vulnerable she would have been.

"That's quite impressive," he said. Scanning the crowd, trying to keep his mind on picking out the possible paparazzi that might be sprinkled throughout. He needed to get his picture in the papers. That was the whole point of tonight, after all. Not to think of Noelle, in front of so many people at such a young age. Exposed to all manner of criticism.

He shouldn't care. But he found that he did.

"Oh yeah, fabulous. I've burned through the career of the lifetime and hit the point of redundancy at twenty-two. Hooray for me."

"Why is it you think you're redundant?" He broke from looking into the knot of people and turned his focus on her.

"Well, let's see. I'm broke. Instant noodles is fine dining in my home and…oh yeah, I just took a position as a man's fake future bride in order to keep myself from having to move into a cardboard box."

"Honestly, I will never be able to fathom women's moods."

Her eyebrows snapped together. "What does that mean?"

"You were fine a moment ago."

"Fine before I found out…" She looked around furtively. "Fine until I found out I was here, at this party, on charity when I was a performer at a party for the same person once. A highly valued one. If it weren't for you the only way I'd be allowed in here would be if I was serving drinks."

"Jealousy, or inadequacy?"

Noelle felt unreasonable anger at Ethan rise up in her. "Why not both?"

He grabbed onto her arm and turned her so that she was facing him, not caring that the wait staff and guests were having to move carefully around them in the crowded space. "I'll tell you something, Ms. Birch. You're here with me. And that means it's not you who should be feeling jealous."

"High opinion of yourself."

He snorted. "You think I'm full of myself? Nah. I'm just realistic. I've got more than a billion dollars. I'm talking sitting in my bank account, that's discounting assets. My family on my father's side is old money, made even richer by the success they've had with their resort chain. And my mother is a former A-list movie star with connections most people can only dream of. Half the women in here would give their favorite handbags to be with me and it has absolutely nothing to do with who I am as person, but what I could give them. But they aren't with me. You are."

It didn't really make her feel better, his little speech. After all, he wasn't here with her because he cared for her. He'd sort of taken her in, like a stray cat. A stray cat who had to earn her milk and catnip by posing as his fiancée. But that was a whole different ball game to being the woman he desired.

But his speech did resonate with her. People wanted him because of what he had, because of his influence, and just like her, if it was all gone tomorrow, his popularity would be too.

And how empty was that? No wonder he was willing to get married to inherit the resort chain. He had to get everything he could to cling to the things that made him special.

It was relatable on a bone-deep level. It was what she wanted too. She was trying to get what she needed back. The things that made people look at her, acknowledge her.

If she couldn't have the fame and the glory she'd accept just not being homeless. She wasn't feeling particularly picky.

"I know all about that, Ethan," she said, taking a glass of champagne from a passing waiter's tray. The time to have a drink was now.

"Do you?"

"Look around us. Look at all the friends I have. Didn't you see my support crew rallying around me back at the house that day you first came? People ready to hold a bake sale to help me hold onto my home? Oh, no, there was no one. Because *I'm* no one. At least as far as everyone else is concerned."

Ethan looked at her, his dark eyes locking with hers. He pressed his palm to her lower back, dipped his head low. Any of the people around them would be forgiven for thinking that he was going to pull her to him and kiss her right there in front of everybody. She didn't think that. She didn't. It certainly wasn't why her lips were dry and her pulse was pounding.

"Let me tell you something, Noelle. It's these people— anyone who believes that. They're the ones who don't matter."

She swallowed hard, her eyes stinging with a sheen of moisture, threatening to turn into a source of real embarrassment. She pulled away from him and looked at the stage. There was a piano there. She wondered who was playing tonight.

Her hands itched all of a sudden. Flexed as she thought of playing a slow, smooth song

Because she couldn't look at Ethan. And she couldn't think about what he'd just said. It was contrary to everything she'd ever been taught about life. About what was important.

And he was just trying to make her feel better, because who wanted a cranky-looking woman on their arm all night?

A woman, a very young woman in a long red dress, came floating out onto the stage and sat in front of the piano, a string quartet sitting down the stage from her. The first strains of the music started to filter through the room and Noelle closed her eyes. Let them fill her with longing, with an ache that she was afraid would never go away.

"Care to dance?"

She opened her eyes and looked at Ethan, his eyes hot and intent on her. She cleared her throat. "You dance?"

"My mother insisted I learn. And anyway, I found it quite instrumental in picking up women back in the days before my bank balance was quite this healthy. Back in the days when I had to rely on charm and skill to get a date."

She looked back at the stage, at the performers. She'd always been the one up there. Separate and removed. The mood of the room. A part of the parties, an integral part, but never in them.

"For the press?"

His lips curved up slightly. "Yeah, of course."

She accepted his offered hand. It was hotter than she'd imagined it would be, his palm a bit rougher. He led her to the dance floor and her heart started tripping on itself. She'd never danced with a man before. She'd never danced. Not even at her own CD-release parties. But she'd even performed at those, even then more the entertainment than the guest of honor. And dancing wasn't essential to piano, which meant it was a skill she'd never acquired.

"I don't really know how to dance," she said, when they stopped at the edge of the dance floor and he pulled her gently into his arms.

"But I do. And you can let me lead." He laced his fingers through hers and wrapped his other arm around her waist. "Put your hand on my shoulder," he said, his voice soft, enticing.

She obeyed the instruction and immediately had to fight the urge to slide her hand, palm flat, down to his hard-muscled chest. She knew it was muscular because her breasts were crushed against it, her heart raging, and she was certain he could feel it.

She looked back up at the stage as Ethan moved back. She felt it all flow through her, the music and his movements, and her feet seemed to obey the prompting from Ethan's body. Everything just seemed to work.

"So tell me, why don't you know how to dance?"

"No time," she said, her words short and breathless, not from the exertion of dancing, but from being in such close proximity to a man. To this man.

"Ah, right. The drills."

"Yeah, the drills. They took up—take up—a lot of time."

"I see."

"A person can't be great at everything. You can be great at one thing, if you work at it. If you want it badly enough." She repeated the words of her former piano teacher, slightly shocked at how quickly the words rolled off her tongue, even after all this time.

"I don't accept that," he said, pressing his hand more firmly against her lower back, moving the lower part of her body closer to his. It made her tingle, made her uncomfortable...aware of her breasts. It was the strangest thing. Not completely unpleasant.

"Doesn't matter whether you accept it, it's true. It takes hours and hours of dedicated practice to claim proficiency at anything. It takes true commitment."

"Hmm, commitment I'm not so good with."

Her pulse pounded harder. He flexed his fingers and the slight motion against her back made a shock of sensation skitter through her veins, lighting up every last part of her body, from her head to her toes and every inch in between.

"Are you sure? Because you asked me to marry you only twenty-four hours after meeting me."

"Commitment with a catch I can deal with. Commitment with a defined end date, I actually think that's quite perfect. But then, that's why I don't make commitments. Because I know I wouldn't want to keep them."

"Well, then your proficiency must be in something other than relationships."

He smirked. "I have a major in business with a pretty accomplished minor in bedroom skills. And I only claim a minor because you insist a person can't have a double major in life."

She felt her face get hot, her blood pounding in her temples. She didn't know how he could say things like that so casually, like it didn't mean anything. As if it didn't throw his mind straight into the bedroom with all kinds of sweaty, half-formed visions.

She'd watched her share of late-night cable when she'd been alone in her hotel room, so she knew what kinds of things he was talking about. And it was making her feel weak and shaky all over.

"What about you? What's your view on commitment?"

"I majored in piano," she said, forcing a smile. "Figuratively speaking, of course."

"Yeah, I got that. I see what you were doing there."

"You're making fun of me," she said. But he wasn't doing it in a cruel way. He was teasing her. She wasn't sure if anyone had ever really teased her like that. If anyone had engaged her in conversation quite like this. Intimate. Sharing. Strange.

"A little bit."

He turned away from her and she couldn't help noticing how striking his face was in profile. Strong nose and square jaw. He was almost too perfect to be real. He was like a man chiseled from rock, only infused with breath and warmth. And a glint in his eye that spoke of sin and pleasure.

"Over there," he said, inclining his head slightly. "That's Anita Blaire, she's the lead writer for the society pages."

Noelle turned her head slightly and saw a woman craning her neck to get a look at them.

Ethan released his hold on her hand and placed his palm on her hip, sliding it around slowly until both of his hands were rested on the indent in her spine, just above her bottom. He moved his thumb slightly, slowly, his touch edging near intimate territory.

She stiffened, her heart pounding so hard she was afraid she was going to pass out. She swallowed, barely able to finish the job thanks to her suddenly dry throat.

"Relax," he whispered. "Lean into me."

She did her best to relax but her muscles were locked up, tense. Not with fear, but with anticipation. She didn't know what he might do next. Where he would touch her. It made her hot and shivery all over. Like having a fever, one that burned from deep inside her core.

"How's this?" she asked, her voice a little bit thin, shaky.

"Better," he whispered, his lips brushing her temple, the slightly intimate caress making her stomach tighten with raw, sexual need. It was different like this. In the arms of a real man, instead of just the hazy fantasy of a dream lover's caress. Her ideas of desire were all viewed through a Vaseline-smeared lens in her mind's eye. But this wasn't obscured or blurred, it was sharp and clear. Almost painful in its intensity.

And he hadn't even kissed her.

Would he? Eventually. He would have to eventually because he would have to do the kiss-the-bride thing at the wedding. And now her palms were sweaty. She tightened her grip on his shoulders.

He angled his head and his lips skimmed the line of her jaw. She blew out a shocked breath and dug her fingernails into his shoulders, just to get that extra hold, because she felt as if she might melt into a puddle of Noelle at his feet. Wouldn't that be a good picture for the society pages?

He pressed his lips more firmly to her skin, just beneath her ear. She shuddered when he brushed the tip of his tongue over the tender skin. She'd never even known to fantasize about such a simple, sensual thing. Even if she had, she wouldn't have known the effect it would have on her.

"You taste like vanilla," he said, his voice soft and husky, his breath touching her neck, making goosebumps spread over her.

She pulled her head back so she could look at him, at his dark eyes, so intent on hers. Was he going to kiss her now? Like, really kiss her?

He looked away from her, back in the direction of Anita. "I think we've caught her attention," he said.

The shroud of arousal that had cocooned them just a moment before broke and Noelle became conscious again of the noise in the room. The buzz of conversation, the music, the fact that there were other people there, in the ballroom, in the world.

"Oh," she cleared her throat, "yes."

"Ready to go and be social?"

No. She was ready to go and crawl under a rock and hide for ten years, thank you very much, because she'd made an idiot of herself over the brief brush of his lips on her skin. The worst thing was, she was still wishing he'd done more.

"Of course," she said, her voice brittle.

"Come on then, sweetheart, let's spread the good news of our new-found love."

CHAPTER FIVE

TOTAL bliss. She was warm. And comfy. Happy even. Cocooned in the thousand-thread-count sheets in a luxury hotel. And room service was on its way up with coffee.

Noelle snuggled down deeper into the bedding and sighed. For a few moments her mind was blank, and then last night came rushing through it. Not just her mind, her body. She could feel him again, his large, warm hands on her hips, his lips against her jaw.

She flung her arm over her eyes and growled into the empty room. She didn't want to be dealing with this at the moment. And definitely not with him. She had to keep it in the realm of business transaction or it was just...wrong.

There was a heavy knock on the door and she tugged the covers up to her throat. "Come in."

"Morning." He brought coffee, but he wasn't room service. Ethan strode in, looking amazing and not at all like they'd stayed at a party until the early hours of the morning.

He was wearing a dark suit and a white shirt that was open at the collar. She could see just a hint of dark chest hair when he moved and the shirt gaped a bit...and she was staring. And it was probably obvious. She looked out the window.

"So you aren't...I was expecting room service."

"I intercepted them. Said I wanted to wish my darling Noelle a good morning in a way only I could."

She felt her face get hot. "You do have a flair for drama."

He chuckled. "I wouldn't say that. But I do want this to work. And in order for that to happen, everyone around me has to believe that you've done a real number on me."

"Do they?" She couldn't really imagine doing a number on a man. Not when his presence made her feel hot and sort of uncomfortable. But not in a bad way, really. Actually, it was the most pleasant discomfort she'd ever felt before.

"So, what's on the agenda for today?" He looked surprised by her question. "What?" She shrugged. "I'm sort of…working for you now. Kind of my job to be at your beck and call."

His facial expression shifted, a subtle change, his lips parting slightly, a dark and dangerous light illuminating his brown eyes. The intensity of his focus only made that discomfort spread through her a little more, from her tightened stomach and pounding heart down to her limbs, to the apex of her thighs.

"Now that is a very interesting and tempting thought, Noelle."

Noelle felt heat creep from her breasts up her throat and into her face. She knew she was pink everywhere. She was usually so pale, her skin always gave her away.

Because she knew what he was thinking. It was the same thing she was thinking. Her mind was back on last night, on what it had felt like to be in his arms. And now here she was, in bed, and it all seemed easy…as if everything might be simpler if she just scooted over and made room for him next to her.

She gulped a too-hot mouthful of coffee and swung her

legs over the side of the bed. The briefness of her nightie was now the least of her worries.

"Not what I meant, Ethan."

"I don't have designs on your womanly virtue," he said, his tone heavy with sarcasm. "Promise. Much too complicated at this stage in the game."

"Agreed," she said, ignoring the heat in her cheeks. *Womanly virtue.* Good grief. If only that wasn't so close to the truth—not that she counted it as a virtue. More like a somewhat telling commentary on just how thoroughly her life had been managed from moment one.

No boyfriends. Not even a hint of teenage rebellion. She'd been too busy. And she'd believed so strongly in everything her mother had asked of her, had wanted to repay her for the years of travel and lessons by doing well.

By doing what she'd been asked, or rather ordered, to do. And now she *was* paying for it, since she didn't know the first thing about real life. She knew about glitz and glamour, but not how to make the money to achieve it for herself. She knew about air kisses and fake praise, but not about real relationships. Real kisses. Ethan had come the closest.

She shivered at the memory.

"Come to work with me?"

"Um…sure." It wasn't at all what she'd had in mind, but then, she wasn't really certain *what* she'd had in mind. "I'm not going to be spending every waking minute with you, am I?"

"I don't know, what would you do if you were head over heels in love? In love enough to get engaged only a couple of weeks after meeting someone?"

She laughed as she edged over to the bathroom, conscious of her semi-dressed state. "I have no idea."

"I don't either, but I imagine that we very much would spend every waking, and non-waking, moment together."

His eyes, so hot on her, felt like an intimate caress. One that made her burn inside. She crossed her arms over her breasts to disguise her nipples, beaded tight against the filmy fabric with no bra to help hide the effect he was having on her.

"In any case, going to work with you today might be… fun."

Ethan gritted his teeth and fought hard against the razor-sharp edge of arousal that was digging into him, cutting into his control. She was barely covered up by a silky, bright-blue confection that looked as though it was designed for the sole purpose of driving a man to an early grave. Or at least to the hospital to see a doctor about an erection lasting longer than four hours…

She wasn't just an easy tumble though. This wasn't about sex, and it sure wasn't about using her body. He didn't need her body. He could have his pick of any woman he wanted. He wasn't about to let her control him, not about to let himself believe the attraction to her was special in any way beyond what was normal. He'd let it make an idiot of him last night. He'd flirted with her. Nearly kissed her.

He just hadn't had sex in so long that his body was trying to convince him she was special. She wasn't. She was just another blonde. Blondes he'd had. Lots of them.

But her legs. So long and shapely, and her figure, petite and luscious, pert round breasts that called out to him. To touch. To taste. He had a feeling that even if he'd satisfied his libido last week—hell, last *night*—he'd feel the same way.

Feel some sort of sick craving to possess her in every way. To make sure the deal went through? No, not even he would stoop that low. This wasn't about her; not about hurting her anyway. It wasn't even about hurting her mother, not on his part, anyway. It was about showing his father that going through life using people as rungs on the ladder of success and satisfaction didn't work.

About making sure Damien Grey wouldn't get rewarded for it.

"Maybe you should go get dressed."

Her cheeks turned pink, a deep rose that betrayed her embarrassment. That was a novelty, one he wasn't sure how he felt about. A woman who blushed like that over something so simple, that wasn't really his thing. And yet for some reason, it made his body harder, more tense, more aroused.

This was a business deal, in a way, and he had to remember that. But he worked with women every day without experiencing this problem. Of course, the women he worked with didn't come into the boardroom wearing silky lingerie.

He ground his teeth together and tightened his hands into fists, channeling his tension into his screaming tendons. He had to get a grip. On his libido or his body, he didn't really care, but the attraction to Noelle had to be managed.

"Right." She slunk off to the bathroom, and he let out a breath he hadn't been conscious of holding.

The office was safe at least. It would give him a chance to remember why he was doing this. Give his body a chance to calm down. Because he had a goal and he wasn't about to let an errant attraction distract him from reaching it.

More importantly, he wasn't about to give in to temptation, to let his body have the control when he despised men who behaved like having testosterone meant they couldn't be their own masters.

He'd watched his father do it, time and again. Disregarding the feelings of his wife, his children, and for what? For the pursuit of his own selfish pleasure. Casting off every last piece of his honor, his commitments, to chase after a woman who, in the end, wouldn't even stay with him.

He looked at the closed bathroom door and tried not to imagine Noelle's nightgown slithering over her curves and pooling onto the floor.

He wasn't his father. And while she wasn't her mother, she was the one woman who was patently off limits.

"You do have a nice office." Noelle leaned back in his office chair, her long legs stretched out in front of her, black tights covering all that tempting, creamy skin, but doing nothing to disguise the shape.

Turned out she was just as sexy when she was fully dressed. Which he'd known after last night, but when he'd invited her to the office he'd imagined she'd put on something more business-casual. He had discovered that ex-performers didn't have much in the way of business-casual. What she did have was a brief, black dress, black tights and a pair of gold high heels that glowed from fifty paces away.

And all that pale blond hair, hanging loose around her face like a halo…she was just impossible to put in a corner and ignore. And that was problematic on many, many levels.

"Gets the job done anyway," he said.

"Is there something I can do?" She straightened, crossing her legs at the ankles. It did not help make her look any more demure.

"You can get out of my chair."

She turned crimson and popped up. "Okay, done. Anything else?"

"You want to work?"

"Well, I'm here." She shrugged. "It seems like I ought to do something. Won't people think it's funny I'm just hanging out?"

"I don't think anyone thinks it's funny at all. I think they assume we're in here not working."

"Oh. Really?"

"Really. Did you see the paper this morning?"

"No, I didn't have the chance to grab it."

"We're the new hot couple, you know."

"Can I see?"

He rounded the desk and leaned over, typing in the web address for the newspaper they'd been featured in. "There you are."

She leaned in next to him, that sweet vanilla scent teasing his senses, making his body harden with tension and arousal.

A small smile curved her lips. "They know my name."

"You sound surprised."

"No one's missed me much over the past year. Which I actually consider kind of a blessing. I haven't really been keen on sharing my downfall with the world."

"What? That your mother stole your money?"

"That she abandoned me because she knew she'd gotten everything she could out of me. Because my sales—album sales, ticket sales—were dwindling to nothing."

"So what have you been doing then, this past year?"

She shrugged again, her blue eyes fixed on a point somewhere behind him. "Nothing."

"Nothing?"

She looked at him, pale eyes filled with anger now. "Maybe I haven't done the best I could with my time. But

I didn't really know what to do. I only know how to do one thing." She looked away. "My mother made sure I only knew one thing. I tried to…I tried to talk to my old booking agent. Tried to see about playing venues I used to play. I called my label and asked them if they wanted to release a greatest hits album. Turns out, they don't think I have any." She laughed, a hollow, bitter sound that made his chest ache. "So in that sense, I did something. But I just…I didn't know what else to do when all of that was shot down."

"What about playing piano bars and things like that?"

"Ironically, that's the kind of thing I am a bit too famous for, and I don't mean that in a snobbish way, I mean…I didn't want that to show up in tabloids."

"That's not really a great excuse, Noelle. You basically just sat there and let everything fall apart."

"No. No I did not. Everything was wrecked, utterly wrecked by my mother. She smashed everything to pieces—I didn't let it fall apart. And yes, maybe I could have done something, maybe I should have, but every night I've gone to bed hoping…hoping that somehow in the morning it would be fixed. That things would go back to normal. I tried to force it to go back to normal." She looked at him, blue eyes intent on his, an impact he felt all the way through his body. "Now…now I don't even want things to go back to normal. But I just…I felt burned out. I was just so tired. This, having a chance to hold onto something, this at least makes me feel like I can fight. Like I have something to fight with."

His chest felt strange. As if it had gotten smaller, or his heart had gotten larger. He didn't like it. "You could learn something else."

Her frame slumped. "I don't know if I have the energy anymore. To devote myself to mastering something other than music, I mean. I've done that. Practicing, improving, every day without stopping since I was a child. It didn't really get me anywhere, did it?"

He didn't know why he felt compelled to try and offer her...something. Comfort maybe? He only knew that he did. "Very few people live their lives that way, Noelle. With drills and practice for eight hours a day, in addition to performing and promoting and traveling."

"Are you telling me you work any less hard?" she asked.

"No, I work a lot. But I choose to. There are plenty of people who go nine to five, five days a week."

She looked down, her throat working. "What if I can't do anything else?"

Everything about his carefully laid plan, her being in the office, her being anywhere near him, suddenly felt wrong. Like he was joining in the queue of people who'd used her.

A bit too late to feel that way.

Much too late. And she was walking in with her eyes open.

"Of course you can. Here," he slapped his palm on the leather back of the chair, "get in the chair."

She sat back down, her expression confused. Damn, but she made him feel every inch the Big Bad Wolf to her Little Red Riding Hood. He didn't really like the feeling.

He shoved his conscience to one side. He'd deal with it later. "Do you type?"

She grimaced. "Not really. Not fast."

"Well, you're going to learn." He pulled out a stack of papers he'd set aside for his PA. "I want you to enter this into the computer. These are specs for different building plans. If you enter the numbers in these cells, the computer will do the math for you. You just enter it in."

"I can do that."

"Okay, do that. I'm going to go down the hall and make some phone calls, and I'll be back to check on you." Distance was definitely necessary.

He walked out of the office and closed the door behind him, his chest still tight. He didn't know why it mattered, but he wanted to show Noelle that she could do something. Something other than doing drills every day for a career that had crumbled to nothing right in front of her.

More than that, he didn't like what he saw in her eyes. That look that said she saw herself as a failure. He'd watched his mother go through that. Watched her pin her self-worth on the perception of a fickle public.

There was no happiness there.

When and how had he started comparing her to his mother? He ought to be comparing her to her own. Actually, the truth of it was, he shouldn't be putting this much thought into her either way. She was just the means to an end, and he was the same to her.

This wasn't personal. Not between the two of them.

He ignored the kick in his gut that said otherwise.

The sense of accomplishment that filled Noelle when she moved the last piece of paper to her finished stack was silly, and she knew it. It had been an easy job, one that she was sure anyone with fingers could do, and yet, it was more than she'd pushed herself to do recently.

She'd been so determined to live in the past. All the time she spent still doing drills she could have used to learn any number of job skills. She simply hadn't. Part of her hadn't believed she could. But Ethan had believed in her. Enough to leave her in his office on her own, to trust her to do the work.

The door to the office opened and Ethan walked in. "I

did it," she said, not quite able to wipe the idiot grin off of her face.

"Good," he said, not half as thrilled as she was.

"Thank you."

The corners of his mouth turned down. "It's nothing. My PA will be happy that she doesn't have to do that today."

"It was something to me."

His eyebrows locked together. "You can do things, Noelle. You aren't stupid. You aren't handicapped in any way. You can do whatever you like. Don't leave it up to the public to decide how much you're worth."

Did she do that? She supposed she had. She'd been so worried about what people might think...that was one reason she hadn't gone and gotten a job. That and the lingering hope that someday she'd be able to fix things.

But she hadn't fixed it yet. And she'd let things get too bad. So much of this had become her fault.

"You're right."

"Yeah, well, of course," he said.

"Really. I could have done something. I didn't."

"Well you can do data entry for me if you like. It's boring, but my PA thinks so too, so she'll be glad to do other things."

Noelle felt her throat tighten and then she just felt silly. Getting emotional over a desk job.

"Thank you."

"It will allow you to be around the office more, which will be good as far as setting the stage for our wedding."

She swallowed. "Yes, it will."

"No working late, though. I plan on keeping you very busy at night."

CHAPTER SIX

KEEPING her busy at night turned out to mean something very different from what she'd immediately thought. She was slightly embarrassed to admit, even to herself, exactly what her first thoughts had been.

But what he actually meant turned out to be something far beyond what she'd imagined.

"Australia?" she asked the next morning when Ethan stopped by. It was good for the staff to see him there, he said. Even better if they just thought he was leaving early after a night of unbridled passion.

"Yeah. I need you to come and meet my family, and in order to do that you have to come to my family's home. Not my parents' home. My grandparents' home. I spent a lot of time there growing up."

"That's…that's really nice." She frowned. "I really don't like the idea of lying to your grandparents."

"I'm sure my grandfather half expects this. He's controlling as hell, but I actually think he means well. He knows I'll do the right thing, or at least the thing he asks of me. Which is more than he's ever got from his own son."

Ethan made it sound as if his parents were a lost cause, but at least he had his grandparents. She didn't have that. Her father, an investment banker from Switzerland according to her mother, had left before her first birthday. And her mother's antics had alienated Noelle's grandparents long before she was born.

She couldn't help wondering what it would be like to have that stability. Any stability.

"Do they…do they know about my mother and your father?"

"Odds are they do. He wasn't exactly discreet."

"Ethan, I'm…"

"Don't."

She stopped the apology from tumbling out and tried not to be too hurt by the hard tone of his voice. She cleared her throat. "But your grandfather…he's good to you?"

Ethan shrugged. "Yeah. He's tough, but that's probably a good thing."

Do it again, Noelle. You're getting sloppy. Why was her mother's voice still so loud? Just the memory of it made her hands ache. She remembered doing scales for hours, so long that she could hardly feel her fingers anymore, so that the action seemed disconnected from her body, divorced from conscious thought.

"Too tough isn't always good," she said, flexing her fingers to try and relieve the phantom pains.

"Too easy isn't good either. No discipline? No control? Makes for a pretty worthless excuse for a human being."

The venom in his tone surprised her. "And too much turns you into a machine repeating the same drills on the piano eight hours a day."

"It's a rare person who has too much discipline, Noelle. But you might fit under the heading."

"You too, Ethan?"

He turned to face her, his dark eyes molten, hot, burning straight into her. "That remains to be seen, I think. Be prepared for my grandmother to grill you, by the way."

She let out the breath she'd been holding and tried to smile. "This is going to be quite the dinner party."

"This may be why I haven't married yet." He chuckled darkly. "My family is far too dysfunctional to inflict on anyone else. Of course, it may be me. If they're as bad as all that, I can't be much better."

"You seem nice to me."

"Well, that's the thing, Noelle, you don't really know me. If you did, you might feel differently. And you aren't marrying me, not really. Not forever." The look that flashed in his dark eyes was strange, pain-filled. It made Noelle's stomach tighten.

"It's all right, you don't know me either."

"It's probably why we get on so well."

She laughed. "Is this your definition of getting on well?"

"We're both still standing." Ethan cocked his head to the side, his expression intense. She could feel his gaze, almost like a physical touch as he looked at her body. Her breasts. She was certain he was looking there because she could feel it. "For now." The air in the room seemed to thicken, a strange electric feeling arching between them as he took a step towards her. Only one step. No more. And she had the feeling that if there was going to be anything more, she would have to make the next move.

Her feet seemed to be rooted to the spot.

"I guess we'll get to know each other in Australia," she said. "Although I think it's kind of a raw deal, you hiring me and then making me ask my boss for vacation time."

"I'll keep you busy," he said, his voice rough. "And yeah, we may get to know each other a little better."

"We won't actually be staying with my grandparents." Ethan turned to look at her as he navigated the busy

Brisbane expressway and took an exit that led off into one of the suburbs.

She could swear that Ethan's accent had thickened the moment they'd landed in his home country. And she liked it. A little bit more than she should. But it was fascinating, being alone with a man like this. It was something she'd never really experienced before. Well, discounting her piano instructor.

"Where will we be staying?"

"One of my hotels. On the beach. I think you'll like it."

"How long have you owned it?"

"It's been there for years, but I bought it and had some renovation done on it about six years back."

"I've been here before," she said, looking out the window at the passing scenery. "I didn't get to see anything. Just the roadway from the airport to the hotel, to the theater, then back to the airport. We went to Sydney after. I didn't get to see much of it either."

"You never went sightseeing when you traveled?"

She bit her lip. "When we were in Europe we did a bit of it, as part of my schooling. I had a good tutor. He made sure I finished my studies early. I graduated at fifteen, so I was able to practice my music more."

"Have you ever concentrated on anything but your music?"

"I've just been concentrating on breathing this past year," she said, watching the deep green eucalyptus trees blur together into a continuous smear of color. "And before that, just breathing and playing. I want to do more than that now."

"Data entry?"

She shot him her deadliest glare, which, she knew, wasn't very deadly. She'd been told she looked like a Kewpie doll more than once. Not very threatening.

"Something more than that maybe even. But it's a good start."

The car pulled up to a massive, wrought-iron gate and Ethan leaned out the car window and punched in a series of numbers. "Gated community," he said. "Nothing but the best, you know."

"I think it's nice." The car wound up a long, winding hill and she knew that Ethan's grandparents' house was certain to have billion-dollar views.

"It's a bit pretentious, actually, but don't tell my grandmother I said that."

"I wouldn't."

He turned to her, sliding his hand across the expanse of seat between them. He laced his fingers through hers, his thumb drifting over the back of her hand. She felt goosebumps raise up on her arms. He hadn't touched her for a long time. Only a few days, actually, and yet…it felt like a really long time.

"I'm going to introduce you to my grandparents and get the family ring from my grandfather after dinner, let him know my intentions and all that."

Her heart slammed against her breast. She nodded, trying to pretend she was unaffected.

"And then I'll give it to you after we leave. We'll have to come up with a nice story for my grandmother because she'll want all the gory details. Women always do."

"Yes. True." Her stomach tightened, a sick feeling spreading through her. "I…I don't know how I feel using your family heirloom ring when it's…when we're lying."

"So? I'll return the ring when our marriage fails. What difference does it make?"

"None, I guess." Except it kind of did. "Why didn't your mother end up with the ring?"

"It wasn't new. She doesn't really like antiques." The

corner of his mouth curved up slightly. "She likes really modern stuff. Spot-on trend. And my grandmother never would have let her put it into a new setting."

"Family traditions shouldn't be broken. I mean, I don't think. We didn't really have any."

It was no use feeling wistful about it. She'd spent so long just wishing things were different. From the moment she'd realized her life wasn't like other girls', she'd wanted something else. More. A connection with her mother that wasn't based on her career.

But that hadn't happened. It had always been about Noelle's career for her mother. About what she could do, what she could get thanks to Noelle's talents. Noelle accepted it now, more or less. Anyway, the charming revelations Ethan had uncovered about her mother made her realize Celine wasn't the kind of woman she wanted a relationship with anyway.

No, she wasn't going to waste time being pouty about what she had and what she didn't have. Not anymore. She was going to take the money, and she was going to get on with her life. She would take her new office skills, or her rediscovered favor with the media, and she would make something of herself, and manage her own money. Without her teacher. Without her mother. Without Ethan.

She was done being played like a puppet. She was in charge now.

"Mine have more to do with status than sentimentality. My mother is new money, you see, so she doesn't understand how special it is to have things that have been passed down. Or so I've heard," he said, his words cut short as they passed through another gate and onto the grounds of an opulent estate with lush, manicured grounds and three fountains stationed right out front, seemingly for the sole purpose of trumpeting that the people who owned the house had money. Bags of it.

Ethan pulled the car through and parked it in the drive. "My grandparents have valet service," he explained dryly.

He got out and rounded to her side, opening the door for her. "Full service," she replied, standing to find herself just about breast to chest with him.

"I'm a full-service kind of guy," he said, his eyes seeming darker, his voice rougher. She wished she knew what he was thinking whenever that happened. Why it seemed like one part attraction, one part anger, and complete confusion.

Her fingers twitched with the urge to reach out and put her hand to his stubbled cheek, to find out how rough it would be beneath her palm. She wanted to. Badly. But she wouldn't. That part wasn't really confusing. But it was crossing boundaries she wasn't here to cross.

No show without an audience. No touching unless someone was around to witness it. Otherwise it would just be a personal indulgence and she wasn't about to go there.

"I have no doubt," she said, turning away from him.

"Ready?"

She started playing Vivaldi's *Four Seasons* in her head, imaging her fingers moving over the keys. Finding her balance, her center and her tempo. "Ready."

"Then let's meet my family."

As always, a family dinner was a formal affair at his grandparents' home. He'd always found it part of their upper-crust, slightly stiff charm. They weren't perfect, and they were hardly suburban normal, but life with Nathaniel and Ariana Grey had been much more functional than life with his parents.

And after his mother's breakdown, this was where he'd

spent most of his time. His father had been too busy, his mother too ill. And as controlling as his grandfather could be, at least he cared.

When it came down to it, he wasn't overly thrilled about lying to them, any more than Noelle was. But no matter how stern his grandfather pretended to be, he'd never had it in him to cut off his only son.

But Ethan had what it took. No question.

He took Noelle's hand in his beneath the table. A subtle gesture, not one of open ownership. The kind that had the appearance of being only for them, something intimate and special, but was really for the benefit of everyone else. The art of performance.

Still, even if it was a gesture meant for everyone else, the feeling of her silky-smooth skin beneath his palm sent shocks of pleasure through him, desire tightening his gut, making his blood hot.

Noelle Birch was slowly driving him crazy. How else could he be getting hard from holding hands, of all things? Hand-holding hadn't gotten him hard when he was fourteen. He had no excuse for the reaction now.

His grandfather's eyes were fixed on Noelle, and Ethan knew Nathaniel had made the connection. Fifteen years might have passed since the affair between Celine and his father had ended, but no one had forgotten.

"How long have you been seeing each other?" Ariana smiled at them both and he wondered whether his grandmother actually hadn't recognized Noelle. Maybe her manners were simply so polished that nothing could tarnish them.

Noelle looked at him, her blue eyes slightly panicked.

"A few months," he said. "Quietly."

"Must have been," his grandfather said. "I haven't seen anything about it in the news."

"I don't always rate the papers," he replied.

"But she would." Nathaniel dipped his head in Noelle's direction.

Noelle cleared her throat and shifted in her seat. "Not always."

"So, Noelle, you used to travel quite a bit." Nathaniel's focus was on her now. "What are you doing with your career these days?"

Noelle shifted in her seat, her fingers tightening around his for a moment. "I'm on hiatus."

A laugh stuck in Ethan's throat.

"Good." Nathaniel nodded. "A woman needs to focus on things beyond a career."

"If she wants to, I suppose," Noelle replied.

The laugh escaped this time. "You'll find Noelle holds to her own opinions," Ethan smiled wryly.

"Good," his grandfather returned. "Doesn't do any good for a woman, or a man, to have nothing outside of a relationship." The look he gave Ethan was pointed.

"No," Ethan said. "It doesn't."

"Drink, Ethan?"

Ethan nodded and stood from the table, leaning in to drop a kiss on Noelle's cheek. He paused just before his lips brushed her skin, her scent halting him for a moment, just a moment, long enough to savor it, to let it fill him. He couldn't define what it was she smelled like, because it was so unique to her.

Her posture went rigid and she turned her head slightly, like she was anticipating the touch of his lips, but dreading it. He cocked his head to the side and skimmed his lips over her jawbone, just beneath her ear.

"I'll be back in a moment," he whispered, trying to ignore the fierce tightening of his stomach.

He followed his grandfather down the hall, dark and

carpeted with a threadbare Aubusson that spoke of age and money, into his study and shut the door. He crossed to the bar and took out two glasses, one for him, one for the old man, and a bottle of whiskey. He added three fingers of the liquor to the glasses and handed one to his grandfather, raising the other to his lips.

"What exactly are you playing at here, Ethan? Noelle Birch? Am I expected to believe this is a happy coincidence?"

Ethan shrugged and took a swallow of his whiskey. "Don't know if I'd call it happy."

"I'm certain I wouldn't call it a coincidence. I know you far too well for that."

"Maybe I'm in love."

"Are you marrying her?"

He nodded once. It was the truth in the strictest sense. He was simply leaving out his plans for what came after the vows. "That's the plan."

"And you'll be faithful to her?"

Ethan set his glass down on the bar top. "I'm not like my father. If I make a commitment, I honor it. I take care of what's mine."

"Now, that I trust. You know if I do pass the company straight to you what a slight it will be to Damien. Your father has been waiting for this all of his life."

"I'm completely aware." He was counting on it.

"He's my son, Ethan, but I'm not proud of what he's become. I want to make sure you do better for yourself. I want you settled before you get wrapped up in running a corporation like Grey's."

"No offense intended, but the one I run now is larger than Grey's."

His grandfather nodded. "True enough. Which begs the question why you want Grey's so badly."

Revenge was the easy answer, one that didn't seem quite right in this scenario. But there were other reasons, more complex. Ones he didn't like to dwell on. Those reasons took him back to being a boy, a boy with nothing. Of no importance to his parents. Barely worth a second glance if they passed him in the hall of their large family mansion.

"Because what you have is never enough," Ethan said. "That's how it is for businessmen. You know that. You always need more."

"I don't really know what it is you're doing here, Ethan." Nathaniel let out a sigh. "Maybe I don't want to know. I just want you to be happy. Stable."

"I'm stable. I know that my marriage to Noelle will make me very happy." If not for the reasons marriages usually made people happy. If they ever did.

"I hope so. I assume you will want your grandmother's ring?"

This was a huge part of making it all look real. "Yes."

"I'll go and get it from the safe."

Ethan ignored the slow burn of guilt that mingled with the alcohol in his gut. Everything was working out now, just as he'd planned. The ring was another piece of the puzzle.

He downed the last of his whiskey, letting the fire overtake the uncomfortable emotion that was swirling in his stomach. Everything was starting to fall into place, and guilt had no part in it.

"You're tense," Noelle commented.

They were about five minutes into the drive from his grandparents' house and he hadn't spoken a word. His hands were locked tightly around the steering wheel, the muscles on his forearms corded, showing his strain.

"Not at all," he replied, teeth gritted.

"You're a bad liar."

He tossed her a quick glance. "I'm not."

"You are."

"I'm not trying to lie."

"Well, then you're a bad liar when you aren't trying to be a good one. You aren't fine, even I can see that, and I'm not really an authority on reading people. You can use my mother as exhibit A on that one."

He hunched slightly and shifted his hands lower on the wheel. "It doesn't thrill me to lie to my grandparents."

She swallowed. "I'm with you. Your grandmother is… she's very kind."

"She always is. She's so stable. Calm."

"Not like my mother at all."

"Or mine."

"Want to tell me about her?"

He leaned his head back against the seat. "Not in the least. You?"

"Don't you already know about her?"

"I know what I saw. She was beautiful. Charming. She had my father under a spell. What did you see when you looked at her?"

Noelle bit her lip. "All of that. She could play this kind of sweet beauty, act a little bit naive so that she could get away with being demanding. But that was an act. She was smart. Smarter than I am, obviously. She used me to make money, and I can't seem to manage that."

"She was dishonest, you weren't. That's not smarter. That's cheating."

"Then what are we doing right now?"

"We're cheating too. But it's for a good cause. Trust me."

She wished she could.

They were quiet again until he turned the car down a winding road that led toward the beach. Noelle unrolled her window and let the salt air and the sound of waves on the sand fill up the interior of the car. It was preferable to that ear-ringing silence.

Ethan pulled the car up to the front of the hotel and left it, keys in the ignition. He got out, slamming the door behind him, not bothering to come around for her door this time. She sat with her hands in her lap for a moment before opening her own door and following him in to the opulent lobby.

Her stomach tightened as she hurried to catch up with him, her high heels clicking on the black marble floors. She looked up at the high ceiling, at the five levels of rooms, each with a balcony that overlooked the massive lobby, ornate carvings on the hand rails with vines growing over them. Like a ruined city that still glittered with riches.

She'd been here before. Stayed here with her mother whenever she performed in Brisbane. It brought so many things back. Every time they'd come, she'd practically been frog-marched through the lobby on her way to the many-roomed suite at the top floor, and, jet lag not even accounted for, had been settled in front of the piano to practice within five minutes of her arrival.

And her mother had gone out, as she always did. To network or whatever it was she called it. And she'd been alone.

"We're staying in the room with the piano, aren't we?"

Ethan stopped dead in his tracks and turned, his dark eyebrows locked together, the heavy tension still radiating from his body. "Yes."

"I've been here. We came to Brisbane quite a bit for a few years and we always stayed here."

There was a strange light in his eyes, something cold. Dark. "Is that so?"

"Yes. I mean, I like it…it's…nice."

"If you'd like to stay somewhere else…?"

She shook her head. "No. It's fine."

She followed him over to the side of the lobby that had a stone wall and water running closely down the side of it. There was a line of elevators with golden doors, the water routed well around them so that people could step inside without fear of getting their designer clothing wet.

"When did you buy this hotel?" she asked, stepping inside the lift behind him.

"A few years ago. The first of my grandfather's hotels that he surrendered to me. My father used to manage it." He spat the last words out as if they tasted bitter.

"I don't even know who my father is."

He turned to her, his eyes hardened into black ice. "There are times when I wish I didn't know who mine was."

It was difficult to hold his gaze when he looked like that, when the remnants of his charming facade fell away and he was all hard, angry male. But she managed it. She'd spent a long time being submissive, doing as she was told and cowering in fear. She didn't want to do it anymore.

"Why?"

"I think he was quite like your mother in many ways. A cheat."

"Aren't we a pair, Ethan? Probably a good thing we aren't getting married for real."

He grunted in what, she assumed, was agreement.

The doors to the elevator slid open after a moment and revealed an opulent gilded entryway, glowing with gold and cluttered with ornate carvings. She couldn't hold back a laugh as Ethan punched in the key code. She was glad to find a reason, any reason, to laugh. To break some of the tension in her. Tension brought on by being here again. Tension from being near Ethan.

"What?" he asked, pushing open the door.

"This whole hotel is so very not you."

"How do you figure?" he asked, holding the door open for her and letting her enter the room first. He must have calmed down because that reflexive chivalry of his had returned.

"You don't strike me as a man who does ornate. Your hotel in New York is much more in keeping with how I see your style."

"Hotels aren't about me. They're about the people who patronize them."

"True." She knew all about that. When she composed music she had to keep in mind what people would want to hear, and yet…pieces of her soul were always there.

She wished that her gift hadn't gone. That aspect of music…it had been so much in her. Woven through her being. To look at the scenery, this gorgeous hotel, and not hear a soundtrack to it was still painful. She didn't know if she'd ever get used to that resounding silence always filling her head now.

It made her body feel foreign to her. Wrong. All of her, every bit, felt wrong. Like being caught off guard by a change in tempo and not quite being able to find the rhythm again, stumbling over notes, breaking the melody so that it was an unrecognizable jumble. It was such a hellish nothing.

She meandered across the plush living area, her fingers drifting over the keys of the piano reflexively as she passed it by on her way to the exterior balcony. She needed air. Space. If only she could escape from herself. Just for a moment.

She opened the sliding door and stepped outside, the cool air from the ocean raising goosebumps on her arms. At least out here she could breathe better. She hadn't gone out on the balcony the previous times she'd stayed here. She'd looked out the windows at the view, had thought about stepping out, but there hadn't been time.

She frowned. Why? It would only have taken a moment. What else had she missed? Small things. Simple things. An ocean breeze. Having friends. Being kissed.

She closed her eyes and relished the feel of the damp wind on her cheeks.

As much as she wanted to blame everything on her mother, she'd been guilty of having tunnel vision. Her mother had pushed it, supported it, but it had been in her. That drive. That obsession. The need to be better, the best. To push a bit harder each and every day.

Was it any wonder it had all deserted her?

She opened her eyes, watched the waves, the whitecaps glowing in the moonlight as they crashed over the shore. Ebbing and surging, soft and hard, fast and slow. Like music. Something she'd never stopped to look at before, not really. She felt a low hum vibrate in her throat and a couple of notes spilled out. A piece of music. Not one she'd heard before. Her heart thundered hard, adrenaline surging through her. It was the first time in a couple of years there had been something, a sound, a note. Anything.

"Thought the night called for champagne. Alcohol of any kind, really."

She turned at the sound of Ethan's voice and saw him standing in the doorway, two flutes of bubbly in hand, his shirt unbuttoned halfway, his feet bare, dark hair tousled like a woman had just run her fingers through it.

Now, this was very, very different than her stay last

time. She swallowed, but despite the moisture in the air, her throat felt dry.

"I won't say no to that."

He walked to where she was standing, looking like every woman's secret fantasy, his dark eyes locked with hers. He handed her a glass and leaned over the railing, touching the edge of his flute to hers. "Cheers."

She lifted hers in mock salute. "Cheers indeed." She took small sip of the bubbly liquid, then cursed it, because champagne wasn't going to help her dry throat. She turned her focus back on the waves. "It must be nice. Having your own success. Having all of this." She gestured to the view.

He shrugged and leaned against the railing. "I don't mind it."

"You still want more, though? Enough to lie to your grandparents?" He shot her warning look. "I'm not judging. I'm involved in this too, aren't I? I'm just asking."

A muscle in his cheek ticked. "It's not about having more. It's about keeping my father from getting it."

"I don't understand why your grandfather would pass it on to him if he was that incompetent."

"It's not about his incompetence, though I guarantee you I'm twice the businessman he is. It's about principles. You can't just treat people like they're there to serve you, with no regard for how they feel, and then get rewarded for it. I won't see it happen."

"Ethan…"

"I won't watch him win, Noelle. Not after the way he treated my mother. It goes beyond the fact that he was unfaithful to her. He took her money, you know. Like your mother did to you. When his father wouldn't give him what he thought he needed to expand his business interests, he siphoned it off of my mother while he was screwing other women behind her back. Or worse, in plain view. Everyone knew how little he respected her." He took a drink of his champagne. "My mother's not perfect, but she didn't deserve that."

Noelle's throat felt tight. "No one does. I…I'm sorry."

He laughed. Cold. Humorless. "Now isn't that ironic? You, apologizing. I thought I told you not to do that."

"Fine. Then I won't. But I am sorry your mother was hurt. But will this…I mean…will it fix anything?"

He knocked back the rest of the champagne and backed away from the railing. "I'm going to bed."

"Instead of talking to me?"

"I didn't ask you to marry me for psychotherapy or companionship, Noelle. I won't start pretending now."

He turned and left the balcony, left her standing there with her heart pounding in her chest, a sick feeling rolling in her stomach. This was pretend, he was right. And it wasn't about getting to know each other, or caring, or anything real.

So why had it started to feel like it was?

CHAPTER SEVEN

It was sort of nice to have a reprieve from Ethan's presence. Noelle spent the day in and around the hotel, trawling the little shops and indulging in a Vienna coffee at a café near the beach. It was decadent in so many ways. No one telling her what to do, and no pressing, horrible worries.

The bubble bath afterwards had been a major highlight too. Relaxing, which was nothing like being with Ethan. Warm and sensual too, which *was* a bit like being with Ethan.

She swore out loud in the empty hotel suite and embraced the rush of satisfaction it gave her. Her mother had used whatever language she wanted, whenever she felt like it, but Noelle had always been bound to protect her image of being a sweet, eternal child. Nothing even remotely adult or scandalous could be associated with her.

In the end, it hadn't helped. She'd grown up. She'd gotten uninteresting.

She flopped onto the couch and put her feet on the coffee table. This was familiar. Nights spent alone in a hotel room. She'd always cherished the time. Time simply to be herself. To eat a chocolate bar and watch a movie showing her what she was missing, locked up in her ivory tower while the rest of the world lived.

She took a bite of her chocolate bar. She was reliving

old times in a way. But there would be no sexy movies. Being around Ethan was messing with her head and she didn't need to encourage her suddenly perky hormones.

The door to the suite opened and Noelle scrambled to get her robe into place so that everything was covered.

"Hi." He walked in and stripped his black tie off in one fluid motion, casting the strip of silk to the floor. It was like something from a cologne commercial—or one of her late-night movie indulgences. The gorgeous man returning home after a long hard day to sweep his woman off her feet and into bed...

"Hi," she replied, hopping up from the couch, holding the lapels of her robe tighter now.

"Good day?"

"I did more data entry. And had coffee."

"All good then?"

"I suppose."

"We've rated the papers over here. Pictures of us getting off my private plane are everywhere."

She took a step toward him. "Do you have them with you?"

"You like being in the news, don't you?"

She shrugged, slightly embarrassed by her enthusiastic reaction. "I got used to it. To watching it. Seeing what people said, what they thought. Good and bad, it all sort of...validated me."

He reached into his laptop bag and pulled out a folded paper. "Enjoy."

She took the newspaper from his hand and opened it slowly, her heart pounding as she looked at the pictures, at the headlines.

Ethan Grey returns home with new squeeze, pianist Noelle Birch, in tow. Meeting the grandparents?

"That's…cool," she said.

"Cool?"

"To get in the pubic eye again like this…like we talked about. But it's more than just showing my mother up. You don't know what this might mean for me."

He didn't smile. His face didn't seem to change at all. But something in his eyes looked different. Darker. "I have an idea."

"You don't approve of my enjoyment of fame?" His silence was its own kind of answer. "My life…the life I had before, it was…It's hard to explain. Parts of it were brutally hard. And yet, there were things that I loved. I loved to play in front of a crowd. I loved it when I would hear the beginning notes of a new song in my head. And I loved when people recognized me. When they were excited to see me. Like they cared or something."

He shook his head, his expression suddenly fierce. "That's not real. None of it is."

"It feels real," she said softly, looking down at the picture.

"Trust me, it's not. Ask my mum how real it is. She was an A-lister for a while. Invited to every party, cast in all the big movies. The public built her up and then forgot about her overnight while she poured everything she had into a husband who acted like she wasn't alive half the time. There's no happiness in seeking the approval of the people. Because maybe they'll give it, but only for a while. And when they take it away, it's a cruel reality."

"Yeah, I'm sort of living that reality, Ethan. I'm aware of how much it sucks."

"All right, Noelle, today your picture's in the paper. What about tomorrow?"

She didn't really want to think about tomorrow. She was safe now. Safe and warm, and feeling pretty happy to be back in the public eye in a positive way. But that attitude was what had gotten her into trouble in the first place. She might be enjoying these snatches of happiness right now—enjoying them too much to see something bad around the corner, something like her mother running off with all her money.

"I don't know."

"No one should have the power to decide how you feel about yourself, Noelle, good or bad. Give yourself that power."

"I suppose it's easy for you."

He shrugged. "I've never cared what other people thought. As long as I'm getting where I want to go, I don't care what other people think of my methods. When you're successful there will always be people waiting to watch you fail. They don't matter."

Ethan's heart was pounding heavily in his chest, a strange, protective sort of anger pumping through him, hot and fast. Reckless. There was no reason he should care, none at all, about the way Noelle saw herself. About the look on her face when she'd seen her picture in the paper.

But it reminded him too much, far too much, of how his mother had reacted to reviews, good and bad, about how she'd been disappointed when the paparazzi had stopped following her. About how thoroughly demolished she'd been when the press had gleefully dissected Damien Grey's appearance with Celine Birch at a major Hollywood industry event, leaving his wife, the movie star, at home.

The constant bitter regret, the desperate wishing that she'd never moved away from California, never sacrificed her figure to give birth to a son who didn't bring her happiness anyway.

Terrible memories of trying to revive her after she'd swallowed a whole bottle of pills.

Putting Noelle in that spot made his gut tighten so hard he couldn't move. Couldn't breathe.

He didn't know why he was doing this, why he was putting her in that place. Why he was feeling things for her.

All he knew was that he wanted to touch her, to comfort her in some way. But the minute he did that, the minute his hands touched her smooth, silken skin, it would be over for him. He would take her in his arms. Kiss her. Seduce her.

No. He wouldn't. He would be in control. Just as he always was. She wasn't different. She wasn't special. He tightened his jaw, clenched his teeth, tried to stop his body's intense reaction to the thought of what it would be like to seduce her.

So sweet. For a moment.

It would almost be worth it.

"What?" she asked, her voice breathless, her breasts rising and falling sharply. She knew. And she was just as affected as he was.

"We'll have more public appearances to make over the coming weeks," he said, his eyes fixed on her full, pale lips. "We have to be sure we're comfortable touching each other."

He took a step toward her, his body urging him on, his mind screaming at him to pull back. He would. He would pull away before it was too late. Just not yet.

Not quite yet.

He put his hand on her cheek, shocked to see how unsteady it was. She was soft, softer even than he'd imagined she would be. And the need to do more, touch more, was so strong it made his body shudder.

"Comfortable?" she asked, her words hushed, her blue eyes wide.

"Not even a little bit. You?"

She shook her head.

"Then we'll have to change that," he said.

He dipped his head and closed the gap between them, pleasure bursting in his stomach, heating him to boiling point, his whole body instantly hard with desire. She tasted sweet, her kiss better than any wine he could remember. And far outstripping any other kiss he'd experienced. He couldn't remember being affected this strongly by the simple touch of lips against his, not even when he'd been a teenage virgin.

A soft sound escaped her mouth and he devoured it, taking the chance to dip his tongue inside, to taste her a bit more thoroughly. Just a taste.

But a taste could never be enough. Not when it made him crave more. Everything.

He raised his other hand and allowed himself to rest it on the indent of her waist, another step into temptation. Another concession. But he would pull away in time. Before it got out of control. There was no 'out of control' for him, he always had it. Always had the power.

She touched the tip of her tongue to his and need shocked him, like a lightning bolt from the point where she made contact straight to his groin.

He couldn't breathe. But it was all right. He would gladly drown in her. In the passion that poured from her and filled him, pushing at the bonds of his control, cracking it, threatening to shatter it.

Was this what his father felt when he was with his mistresses? A pull, a need that felt essential as air?

The thought was a bucket of ice water to his overheated libido. He pulled away from her, his throat tight, his lungs burning with the need to draw a breath he couldn't quite manage to pull in.

"That's enough, I think," he said, his voice rough.

She looked dazed, dizzy. A lot like he felt. "I…"

"Don't worry about the press," he said. "I've got work to do, so I'm going to go to my room now."

He turned without looking at her again. Because if he did, if the look in her eyes reflected the longing he felt, if he caught her scent, he would be lost again.

He couldn't afford that. It was a matter of keeping his focus. And it was a matter of pride. He wouldn't lose either.

Notes moved through her. Music, a melody, vague and unstructured. Noelle turned over in bed, felt the cool sheets against her bare legs. The chill didn't last long. As soon as her thoughts came into sharper focus, she remembered the kiss.

Ethan's lips moving over hers, so expertly. So sensually.

Her first kiss. And it had been…it had been so much more than she'd imagined it could be. All fire and need. Exciting. Terrifying. It had brought something out in her that she hadn't felt before, something she hadn't realized lived in her.

She sat up and swung her legs over the side of the bed, her toes digging into the plush carpet. She could feel it swelling in her, moving through her. It made her ache. Or rather, it added to the ache that was already centered in her chest. An ache that was physical as well as emotional.

It was as if everything was changing, shifting beneath her feet. Not like the cold shock of change that had happened when her mother had disappeared with her money, but something else, something more subtle, but even more dangerous in some ways.

She was starting to feel changed, rather than simply feeling that her life had changed around her. She felt more power. More control. And less, at the same time. She wasn't sure how that worked exactly.

She closed her eyes again, found the melody she'd heard in her sleep. Vague still, but present. Inspiration that felt familiar, like something she used to feel before. She stood, excitement flooding her, and walked through her room, out into the main area of the hotel suite. It was automatic, sitting at the piano, her fingers resting lightly on the keys.

She could still feel Ethan's lips on hers, the hot press of his hand on her waist.

She pressed one key down. Low. Soft and tentative at first. Then she added another. Several joined together, the strains harmonizing, creating a haunting dissonance that filled the room, that reflected the feelings swirling inside of her. Minor. Confused. A little bit sad.

"What are you doing?"

She halted her movements and looked up. Ethan was there, wearing only a pair of jeans resting dangerously low on his hips, revealing lines that led to a part of his body she definitely shouldn't be thinking about. She shifted her eyes up and it was really no better. His chest was art, his abs a sculpture. Every inch of his body was well-defined, dusted with just the right amount of dark hair. Sexy beyond all reason.

"Playing." She forced the word out around the lump in her throat.

"Not a drill."

"No."

He walked closer to her, resting his forearm on the closed top of the shiny black grand. "Not a piece I recognize either."

"Original," she said. And as she said it, she realized it was. It was a song. And it had come from her.

Her stomach tightened.

"I liked it. What was it?"

"I don't know," she replied. Because it was true. She wasn't sure what she felt. What she wanted.

He circled her, moved so that he was standing behind her. He stretched one arm forward, brushing her bare shoulder as he did, resting his fingers on the keys, pressing a few of the them.

"Why not?" he asked, his breath fanning over her cheek.

"Because I'm not sure what I want. Where I'm going. But I want to. I think that's what the song really is. It's longing."

"What is it you long for, Noelle? Fame?"

"I thought so," she whispered. "I'm not sure now."

"Something else?" He put his hand on her shoulder and brushed her hair to one side, exposing her neck, his skin hot against hers.

"Maybe." She sucked in a sharp breath.

"Something with a little bit more…immediate gratification?"

His lips were near her ear, brushing against her, his voice soft, husky, an invitation to sin. She wanted to accept. Regardless of the consequences, in that moment, she wanted to turn and press her mouth to his. To have another taste of the passion she'd been introduced to earlier.

But she didn't think she could take that step. What if he pulled away? What if he didn't want her? She wasn't sure she could handle more rejection, even if it was only physical rejection.

He moved his hand over the back of her neck, the tips of his fingers gliding over her skin. She shivered, her nipples tightening, arousal trickling through her, thick and sweet like honey, making her ache for more.

She knew exactly what it was her body wanted. And she also knew that Ethan could give it to her. It was the other stuff, the heart-pounding, stomach-tightening emotion that frightened her.

The touch of his lips against the curve of her neck made the butterflies in her stomach disperse, letting desire take over. There was no place for fear, not when his touch made her feel so good. So warm.

He kissed her again, a featherlight touch on her shoulder that echoed all through her body. She leaned into him, against his hard body, his bare chest hot against her back. He gripped her shoulders, his hold keeping her from melting into a puddle and sliding down the piano bench.

He moved one hand to her shoulder and brushed the strap of her silky top aside.

"I just want to see," he said, his voice tight. He moved her other strap aside and she felt her top fall, revealing her breasts. The only light in the room was the silver glow of the moon pouring through the window.

Ethan's unsteady breathing, the slight tremble in his hand as he slid his fingertips down her arm, made her feel powerful, made her feel confident in a way she never had before.

"You're more beautiful than I imagined. And I imagined you would be stunning."

She tried to ignore the tightening in her throat, tried to focus only on the desire that was coursing through her. The physical. She didn't want anything else. Didn't need it. She just wanted him to touch her. She didn't know what she wanted after that, wasn't sure if she was ready for more, but if he would just touch her...

"I need to touch you."

"Yes," she breathed.

Permission seemed to be what he'd been waiting for, because the moment the word left her lips, he moved his hands to her breasts, cupping her sensitive flesh, skimming his thumbs over her hardened nipples.

"Oh, Ethan…" She let her head fall back against his stomach and focused on nothing. Nothing beyond the sharp, overwhelming darts of pleasure that were piercing her body, making her ache for more.

She could feel the evidence of his desire, hard and hot behind her. It made her wish she knew what to do, made her wish she had some experience with men so that she'd know how to please him, make him feel even half of what he made her feel with the slightest stroke of his hands on her skin.

He kissed her neck again, more firmly this time. She angled her head and pressed her mouth to his. Passion and fire exploded between them, the heat tangible, enough to burn her inside and out. And she liked it. A lot.

His tongue slid over hers, and she met him, thrust for thrust, tasting him, devouring him as he continue to tease her breasts with his talented hands.

She turned around, still on the bench, rising up on her knees and winding her arms around his neck. He braced his hands on her hips, holding her to him, her bare breasts pressed tightly against his chest.

He nipped her lip, and the shock of the pain, slight but intense, made her heart pound faster, made her internal muscles tighten. She pulled her lips away from his, trying to catch her breath. He kissed her throat, her collarbone.

More. She begged him silently. She wasn't ready to ask out loud. She didn't think she could. But she wanted it. Wanted his mouth on her breasts. She wanted him…all of him.

"Oh, Ethan…" His name seemed like the only thing she could say. Because it was all that filled her mind.

He froze, his hands tight on her still. He pulled his

mouth away from her. His chest was rising and falling sharply, his dark eyes unreadable in the dim light.

He shook his head. "This shouldn't have happened. This can't happen."

The rejection cut into her, clearing the fog of arousal quickly and brutally. "What?"

"Not now. Not with you." He pulled his hands away from her and she wobbled on the bench, bracing herself on the piano keys. The sound of incompatible notes was horrible and far too loud, jarring her the rest of the way back into reality.

"Not with…"

He turned away from her and walked back into his room, shutting the door behind him.

She could only sit there, stunned, not so much by her own behavior, but by his. He wanted her, she knew he did. No matter what he'd said.

Not with you.

Because of whose daughter she was? Or because she wasn't sexy enough? Or for some other reason he'd chosen to invent? She curled her hands into fists and fought the urge to pound them on the piano keys. To make so much noise that he wouldn't be able just to walk into his room and shut her out.

She was angry, embarrassed. But not destroyed. It was funny, she'd felt changed earlier, and now she realized that she really was. Because the old Noelle would have curled up in a ball and hidden after suffering something like that. Or she would have frozen, pretending things would somehow magically get fixed.

But she wasn't hiding now. She had a house to get back. She was strong enough to get through this, and she wasn't going to let something like errant attraction—or rejection—stop her from achieving her goal.

If Ethan didn't want her, that was fine. She would deal with it. And she wouldn't make the mistake of giving in to desire again.

CHAPTER EIGHT

NOELLE had been like a living flame to the touch. Her skin so soft, her breasts the perfect weight in his hands. It had been hell to leave her. Hell to turn away from her when he'd wanted nothing more than to lift her onto the piano and settle between her thighs. To lose himself in her body.

Twelve hours later and he was still so turned on, his teeth ached. And it was the wrong time to be so distracted. And she was absolutely the wrong woman.

It was like a cosmic joke that his body responded to her. Actually, *responded* wasn't a strong enough word—a response was expected between a man and a woman. No, this was…combustion. And it made him feel on edge and out of control, both things he hated.

He gritted his teeth and tried to fight the arousal that still pounded through him. Part of him didn't want to fight it. Part of him wanted to embrace it. To sink back into the dark sensuality that Noelle seemed able to create around them with such ease.

No. Not happening. This was complicated enough without adding sex to the mix. He could control his desire for her, and he *would* control it.

He walked out of his bedroom and into the main area of the hotel suite. It was empty, and he wondered if Noelle was still in her room. And if she was wearing that same, brief nightgown she'd been wearing the night before. She seemed to have a collection.

He could feel his body hardening, his erection pushing against the seam of his jeans, and he tried to reroute his thoughts. Spreadsheets. Spreadsheets and the falling value of real estate. That wasn't sexy at all.

But Noelle still was, and he couldn't shake the image of her from his mind.

He stepped down to the piano and looked outside. She was out there on the balcony, a stack of documents on the table in front of her, alongside a cup of coffee—a vanilla latte, he assumed—and the laptop he'd packed for her.

He slid open the glass door and walked out into the warm coastal morning, relishing the slight bite of the salt air in his throat when he breathed in. Relishing even more the scent of her as it caught in the breeze and teased his senses.

"Working?" He looked at her intently, taking everything in. The way her brows knit together with concentration, the way her fingers moved over the keyboard as they had over the keys of the piano the night before...

Just thinking about the night before made his erection throb.

"Yes," she replied, not looking at him. Her posture was still, her manner cool enough to cut through the Brisbane temperatures. A pink flush spread from her cheeks down her neck. He was starting to wonder whether she actually wasn't that experienced with men—an idea that completely contradicted what he knew about her mother, and what he'd imagined it would have been like for her growing up.

But that blush. Those eager, honest responses...

No. He wasn't letting his thoughts go there again. *That way madness lies.*

"I appreciate it, but you don't have to. I can do that. Or it can wait until we're back in the States."

She kept her eyes fixed, very decidedly, on the computer screen. "No. It's nothing. I mean it's something. It's part of my job, right?"

"Not really."

"You told me that…"

"Yeah, I said you could do it, and you can, but it's not what I need from you."

The flush on her face darkened, and she turned to face him. "Oh. And what exactly is it that you…need from me?"

A few days in his bed. Uninterrupted. Room service brought to the door so they could just forget the world. Just for a while. That idea was more tempting than it ought to be.

Unsatisfied desire made his tone a little rougher than he intended. "What we discussed in the beginning. My priorities haven't changed. I assume yours haven't either."

She looked away again. "No."

"Good." He sat down in the chair across from her. "Last night…"

"I know what it was."

"You do?" Because he was starting to wonder whether he knew. And he knew.

"There's tension between us. We'd be lying if we pretended there wasn't. So it was a…tension…relieving… thing."

"Oh yes, I feel much less tense," he said, fighting the urge to reach back and work the knotted muscles on his shoulders.

"So do I."

"Liar."

She turned to face him again. "You were the one who… stopped it."

"It was the right thing to do, Noelle."

"I know."

"You know?"

She nodded. "Of course. Sex complicates things. And sex between the two of us would get more complicated than things have a right to be. I'm glad one of us was thinking straight. I just want to get through this and get what I need. My house. That's all I really want from you."

It wasn't all she'd wanted from him last night. He was sure of that. She'd been with him every step of the way, no doubt. And today, if not for the blush, he would've assumed she didn't remember that it had happened at all.

"And don't worry, I'll be able to put on a show for the press. What happened happened, and it doesn't change anything. It certainly doesn't change my expectations."

"It doesn't?" Because his body's expectations now seemed radically altered.

"Even if it did, I would do my part. I've always been a good actress."

"You were a musician, you weren't an actress."

She looked past him, her blue eyes unfocused. "Sure I was. I would spend the whole day rehearsing, until the sides of my thumbs bled from scraping against the edges of the piano keys. The whole time my mother would scream at me to do it better. Cleaner. More precise. My teacher would pace the floor and try to run interference between the two of us. When I was a teenager I started yelling back. I would get slapped. And then, after all that, I would go on stage. And I would smile and I would play like I didn't have any troubles. I *am* an actress, Ethan. Better than most you'll find in Hollywood."

She stood up and closed the laptop. "I need to shower."

He grabbed her wrist and held her still for a moment, his stomach tight, sick. "Clearly, the affair with my father was the least of your mother's sins." She looked away from him and he took her chin between this thumb and forefinger, directing her attention back to him. "What happened to you wasn't right. It wasn't normal. You don't have to live that way."

He wasn't so dumb that he hadn't realized Noelle wasn't her mother. It had become obvious after only a few days in her company. But he'd never imagined it could have been like that for her. Had never fathomed just how much she'd been controlled.

Noelle nodded slowly. "I know that's not how it's supposed to be. But I'm not really sure how I *am* supposed to live."

She left the terrace and went back inside the suite, sliding the door closed behind her.

"What was one thing you weren't allowed to do?"

Noelle jumped when Ethan strode into the main area of the suite, and her heart leapt up into her throat. After last night, being around him was… She wanted to turn and run from him or climb him like he was a tree. Which instinct was stronger greatly depended on the moment.

"When I was younger?"

He nodded. "Yes. What was one thing that your mother wouldn't let you do? Something frivolous that has nothing to do with piano-playing or performing or milking you for cash."

A whole lot of things rushed through her head. Shopping. Movies. Dating.

That thought reminded her of last night. Made her body hot all over. The way he'd touched her, the things he'd made her feel…amazing didn't even begin to cover it. But then he'd rejected her. *Her.* Not just sex, but her specifically.

She wished she knew why. She also wished she didn't. And she wished he wasn't so determined to make it up to her. Because she was certain that's what this was: a Band-Aid for the boo-boo he'd inflicted by turning away from her.

He would need a much bigger Band-Aid than a day out to erase the sting of that humiliation. Yet, perversely, she still wanted to be with him. To be near him. To spend the day with him.

"Nothing," she said.

"There was nothing you weren't allowed to do?"

"No. I mean…I was never allowed to just do nothing. Even now, I practice all the time. And what for? For concerts I'll never give? I was never allowed to have a day that was just mine. If we ever shopped it was for my mother, wherever we ate, that was for her too. We never went to the beach because she hated getting sand in her shoes."

"Then that's what we're doing today."

"What?"

"Nothing. Nothing and everything. Whatever you want."

That conjured up images of his hands on her body, his lips against hers. Why she still wanted that after he'd made it very clear he didn't was beyond her. Silence filled the room along with a tension so thick she was pretty sure she could eat it with a spoon.

"Ethan," she said slowly. "Why are you doing this?"

"Because I want to. Because maybe I need to do nothing too." He looked as confused by that as she felt.

"So we'll do nothing then."

"Sounds like a plan."

Noelle looked down at her vanilla ice cream melting steadily in the sun. She'd been sitting in front of the ocean, watching the waves crawl up the shore, then recede, while she indulged in her frozen treat.

Ethan had gone off to take a call, and she finally felt like she could breathe.

The whole day had been…well, it had almost been fun. And would have had zero value as far as her mother was concerned. They'd taken a walk through a historic beach town, eaten lunch at a small fish and chip shack, then got ice cream at a shop right on the ocean.

Perfection. Not exactly relaxing the way she'd hoped it might be, but being near Ethan just wasn't. It ramped her up, made her feel like she was on high alert, made her skin feel extra sensitive, like her blood was flowing closer to the surface. Like everything was more real and more fantastic all at the same time.

"I'll take some of that ice cream." Ethan returned holding two water bottles, looking sexier than any man should in a pair of sandals and some board shorts. He sat next to her and she fought the urge to move closer. Or scoot away. She wasn't sure which she wanted more. So she stayed where she was.

"You had yours. You ate it too fast," she said, licking a drip from the side of the cone.

"And yours is melting. You need help."

She laughed. "I assure you, I don't." She lapped at another drip.

"While I love watching you do that, my professional opinion remains the same." He smiled and she had a vision of the charming playboy she was certain he could be. But behind that, deeper, there was a flicker of heat in his eyes that went beyond simple flirtation.

"I…"

He leaned in and her heart stopped. He was so close

to her, close enough that if she just dipped her head, she could brush her lips against his.

He moved first, angling his head, but not the way she'd been anticipating. He took a long lick of her ice cream cone before leaning back again. "Thanks," he said, his voice rough.

Her hand was shaking from anticipation. From the fact that watching his tongue sliding over the ice cream had actually been pretty hot. She didn't know herself right now.

No. That wasn't true. She was getting to know herself. A sexual encounter on a piano bench and an ice cream cone on the beach at a time. It was like finding out there was a whole different side to herself when she'd always thought there had only been one. She'd been all about the piano. All about performing. But this was living. Real living.

"This has been…this has been great. Thank you," she said, still trying to catch her breath from the sexual shock of watching him lick her ice cream cone. "Sorry I unloaded on you earlier. About my mother."

"We all need to let it out sometimes."

"We both lost the parent lottery, didn't we?"

"Seems so."

"Will you be happy when you get the resorts? I mean, will that be it? Will you win?"

"Is that a trick question?" he asked.

She shook her head. "Not a trick. I'm really wondering. Because I want my…I want my life back, Ethan. Not exactly like it was. I want beach days. But I also want to perform. I want the recognition, the hard work, the reward. The money. I don't…I don't know what to do without it, and I have to believe that if you have a goal like that, when you reach it you'll be satisfied."

Ethan looked toward the sun glinting off the crystalline waves, his brow furrowing. "I don't know the answer

to that. I don't really care. I'm more than happy to keep
fighting for the next thing. Bigger and better."

"That sounds…exhausting."

"More exhausting than doing piano drills for the rest
of your life?"

"Infinitely more."

"There's not really anything more to life, Noelle. You
keep going, you get more. I doubt you'll be satisfied just
playing again. How many people do you need in the auditorium, and after you fill up a large one, won't you need
a stadium? That's how it works."

"I don't…" Noelle's voice trailed off. She didn't like
what he was saying. Because it was frighteningly close to
what she feared might be the truth. That there would be
no satisfaction in 'reclaiming' her career. That she would
get back to that life and find it as empty as the one she
was living now. "I don't believe it. I won't need more. I'll
be happy sitting at the piano, playing."

"Maybe you think sitting at the piano will satisfy you.
But then, you do know how to have fun on a piano bench,
don't you?"

His words hit her like a physical blow, the sudden venom
in his tone shocking her. She stood, brushing sand off the
back of her shorts. "Why would…why would you say that
to me?"

"Noelle—"

"I want to go. Today was…fun. And it was neat to kind
of play hooky from life. But we both have a plan. And
hanging out on the beach just isn't in it."

He nodded. "Not for either of us."

"I don't think hanging out on piano benches is in it for
us either." She turned and headed back to the path that
led to the teeming boardwalk area. A little noise would

be good. A little something to keep her mind off the raw wound in her chest.

How could he say that? As if she let men touch her like that all the time? Though, he might think she did.

Well, so what if she did? She knew *he* was an epic playboy, and if she wanted to get off with men on piano benches every other night of the week that was her business. Not her mother's and not Ethan's. Hers.

She whipped around and was not that surprised to find Ethan only a couple of paces behind her. "You know what, Ethan? It's none of your business what I do in my spare time. Beyond this little charade of ours, my life is none of your business. I could have had sex with a hundred guys, and guess what? Not your job to judge. I'm the one who has to live my life. The one who has to live with me. So… there."

She turned again and walked away, her heart pounding hard in her head, her entire body shaking. It was true, and she hadn't even realized it until she'd said it.

She had to live her life. No one else. Why had she always taken the path other people put her on? Why was she still doing her drills for hours every day?

It was *her life*. No matter how much her mother had wanted to treat it as her own, no matter how much her instructor had fed his ego on her success. They had had no right.

She was angry now. Not just about her situation, but for herself. For everything she'd accepted, her whole life, because she'd believed that her only option was to do as she was told.

Ethan's firm grasp on her arm stopped her in her tracks. He didn't seem at all concerned by the people walking by, craning their necks to see if there was going to be a huge fight between them.

"You're right, Noelle, it's not my job to judge you. And I don't. My comment was out of line." His dark eyes blazed with an intensity that stood in direct opposition to his apologetic words.

"Really?"

"Really."

"I…you apologized," she said.

"Yeah."

"I don't think anyone has ever apologized to me."

"I'm a confident guy, Noelle, and that means my ego can take it when I have to admit I'm wrong. That *was* wrong. It isn't my business how many men you've slept with, or intend to sleep with. It was my sexual frustration talking there. A bit of jealousy, which, I'll be honest, is unfamiliar to me."

"The…jealousy or the sexual frustration?"

"Both."

"Oh." She looked around at the people, moving around them now as though they didn't exist, no more interesting than the pylons that divided the boardwalk from the sand.

"You sound shocked."

"I don't think I've ever aroused either emotion in a man before. So, yes, I am a bit shocked. Maybe as shocked as you are."

"Not possible. I'm sure you make men feel like this all the time."

He looked at her, his dark eyes intense, his jaw shifting as he tightened it, his Adam's apple bobbing.

"I…I doubt it."

He stepped closer, the hand on her arm gliding up to her shoulder, around to the back of her neck, his thumb moving over her skin, fingers sifting through her hair.

"I don't. Not for a moment. You really are beautiful."

"Ethan, I thought we decided that…it's a bad idea." She

hated that. Why was it a bad idea? Ethan felt good. And warm, so warm. Everything had been frozen over for so long, dead and dry. Ethan was like the sun.

She wanted to bathe in his warmth, in the promise of new things that seemed to come every time he touched her.

But it was a bad idea. They'd decided that. She'd agreed.

She moved closer to him, her heart pounding. His hand was still on her neck, massaging her, spreading heat and fire through her.

She didn't want to move away. Didn't want to break her connection with him. It was her life. And she had to live it.

She wanted a little bit of Ethan in it. For as long as she could have it. Because he made her angry and happy and he turned her on. He made her *feel*, when for so long she'd simply been existing. He made her aware of things—needs, desires she'd never been mindful of before.

It was like finding a new dimension to life. And that was more than just the beach and sand and ice cream. It was deeper, it made everything seem as if it had broader scope, more depth.

She didn't want to run from that. She wanted to dive into it head-first.

She stood up on her toes and leaned in, brushing his mouth with hers, her entire body trembling as she increased the pressure of the kiss, as the shock of his flesh on hers fired through her, charging her like a bolt of electricity.

It didn't satisfy her. Not even close. She felt like he was water and she had been lost in the desert. She felt insatiable. She touched her tongue to the seam of his lips, explored the shape of his mouth, tasted his skin.

They hadn't kissed enough last night. He'd done the

touching, he'd done the pleasuring. But she wanted more than that. She wanted it all.

A short groan vibrated in his chest, and he locked his arm around her waist, pulling her to him, holding her against his hard, well-muscled body. She arched into him, could feel the heavy weight of his erection against her stomach.

And that was when she realized they were standing on the boardwalk, in broad daylight.

She pulled away from him, blinking hard. Pushing shaking fingers through her hair, she looked around, trying to see if they'd caught everyone's attention. No, there were one or two people in line for ice cream who hadn't noticed them. Great.

"I...for someone who was trained not to draw the wrong kind of attention, I seem to be doing a pretty bad job at... not drawing the wrong kind of attention."

"You kissed me," he said.

"Not...not *your* attention. People are staring," she hissed, lowering her face and walking back toward the hotel.

"Isn't that the idea? We are supposed to be an engaged couple."

"That wasn't the idea...just now. For me I mean."

"I see, then what was it?"

She stopped and put her hands on her hips. "If you were a gentleman, you wouldn't ask."

"I didn't say I was a gentleman."

"No. I guess you didn't."

"You're right." He sighed. "This is a bad idea."

A bolt of panic hit her in the chest. "Not the whole deal, just the kissing, right? Because I need this, Ethan. I need my house. I can't lose it."

He frowned and reached his hand out, brushing his

thumb over her cheek. "Your cheeks are pink. You need sunblock."

"Please tell me you don't mean the whole deal," she repeated.

"I think it's all a bad idea, Noelle. But I'm not backing out of it. We have a deal, and we'll stick to that. But it's a business deal, don't forget that."

"I...I won't." Of course, if she really felt like it was a business deal her heart probably wouldn't be beating so erratically, and her lips wouldn't still be stinging from the kiss. "We should probably go."

They were still standing in the middle of the crowded boardwalk, but even with so many people everywhere, she felt as if they were the only two people on the planet. At least, the only two who mattered. She wasn't sure what that meant, or why he could make her so mad, and then make her want him, then make her nearly melt inside with the things that he said, all in the space of a few moments.

"Yeah, I've got some work to do this evening," Ethan replied.

"Oh. Good." That meant they wouldn't have time to spend together and maybe she could figure out what was happening inside her. Newfound feelings, along with life-changing revelations, needed to be examined after all. "I mean...I'll have a chance to play around with that song I started working on last night."

A spark crackled between them. The shared memory of what had interrupted her songwriting. His lips on her throat, his hands on her breasts...

"You should wear this." He reached into the pocket of his shorts, took out a small velvet box and handed it to her without opening it. She curled her fingers around it, holding it firmly closed like there was a great hairy spider inside, instead of what she knew was a giant heirloom engagement ring. Actually, at that moment, the ring seemed scarier than a spider.

"You going to open it?"

"Later," she said. Not now. Not on the boardwalk with people all around. Not while she felt scrubbed raw from everything that had happened over the past week.

He nodded once. "We'll fly back to the States tomorrow. Things will settle down. Get back to normal."

She nodded in agreement and tightened her hold on the box. She didn't ask him what he meant by normal, because she was starting to wonder whether she'd ever experienced normal. This wasn't normal. Kissing a man in public, then screaming at him, then having him give her a ring. Marrying him for a house. No, this wasn't normal.

And what she felt for Ethan had even less to do with normal than their marriage farce did.

She'd been expecting that performing, playing for crowds again, being famous and staying in posh hotels would make her feel like herself again. Now she wondered if that had ever been the case. She was starting to wonder if she'd ever figure out what it was she wanted.

She looked at Ethan's strong profile and tried to ignore the tightening in her stomach. All right, so there was one thing she wanted. But it was the one desire she should probably ignore.

Ethan had been wrong about New York bringing normality back. Waking up in the soft, luxurious bed was still too good to be *her* normal. Having Ethan to talk to every day, even if it was about mundane things, was better than normal too.

It was like having a companion, if not almost a friend. Someone to share things with. The details of her day. Three days a week she went to work with him and shadowed his assistant, learning different, somewhat menial office tasks. But she made a mean pot of coffee now and her typing was getting a lot faster than it had been that first day.

And yesterday, Ethan hadn't come by the suite to pick her up in his car, so she'd simply called his assistant and asked her to come and share a cab. It felt…good. As if she was building a life. A *real* life—*her* life—not just the broken remains of a life that had never been hers in the first place.

Ethan was due to arrive, and she was pacing, trying to shake off her nervous energy, fairly certain it was futile. Even after a month with him, even though it had been three weeks since he'd kissed her, she just couldn't relax around him.

She crossed the room to the piano and slid her fingers across the length of the keyboard. Excitement fired through her veins, her stomach tightened in that way that it did when Ethan touched her. Desire. A thrill. She'd been working on the song that had grabbed hold of her in Brisbane, but it hadn't progressed easily. It was still harder to write music now than it had been.

She sat down on the bench and put her hands into position, flexing her fingers for a moment before pushing down on middle C. She added E and G and let the chord fill the empty room, let it fill her.

Then she followed the feeling. She saw Ethan, remembered how he had stood behind her that night back in Australia. How he'd touched her. She hadn't let herself think of it, if at all possible, since their return to New York. But she opened her mind up to it now.

It was easy to put the feeling into her music, effortless. This wasn't like the songs she'd written a year or more ago. Those songs had been born out of technical ability, mostly because she'd had to tame her creativity to make her teacher happy with the structure of a piece.

But this one held her. Her as she was, not beaten into submission, into a shape and form that her teacher deemed salable. Here and now, she was pouring out her feelings, dissonant and minor, filling the room. Uncertain but powerful, deep and all-consuming.

It didn't empty her of the emotion, but made it stronger, growing inside of her, flowing from her fingertips.

She didn't know how long she played, how many times she went through the piece so she could cement it in her mind. When she stopped she sat frozen, before letting it all overtake her.

She felt one tear slip down her cheek, then another. She put her hand over her mouth to cut off the sharp sound that was trying to escape. And then she stopped. She let it all happen, because she'd never done that before. She'd been trying to hold on. To her past, to a life she wasn't certain she would have chosen for herself, but one that she'd been comfortable with.

And she'd never let herself truly grieve the loss of it. She'd never moved on. She'd cut off everything inside of her instead, and she'd lost her music. Not the crowded auditoriums and the CDs, but the music that had always lived in her, coloring the way she saw and heard the world.

It had been quiet in her when before it had always been filled with a rich, layered sound. Music.

She was finding it again. But different. On her terms.

"Are you all right?"

She turned around on the bench and wiped her cheeks, trying to hide the evidence of her crying jag. "I'm great."

"You don't look great." Ethan, who did look great in his custom-made suit, stepped further into the room.

"Gee thanks, Ethan."

"Why were you crying?"

"I have a song," she said. And it sounded lame. It made sense in her head, but she imagined that Ethan probably wouldn't get it.

"Did you finish the one you started back in Australia?" he asked, his voice rough. That pesky, shared memory again. She knew he was thinking exactly what she was thinking.

"Kind of. It was sort of a take-off from that. But it was... different too. I think I might really have something though. It's been such a long time since... I've been able to do drills, songs I knew, but there was nothing new and...that made me feel like part of me had been cut off. Music has always been in me. That's how it all started. I was composing music from such an early age and...my mother saw potential that needed to be capitalized on."

"So it was lessons for you then?"

"With the very best instructor. Neil was—is—a genius. He was my support system until...until my mom ran off with all the money and it was clear I couldn't...pay him anymore."

"After so many years?"

"He gave up everything, every other pupil, for me. And it turned out my mother hadn't paid him in two years. In the end, he just couldn't stay anymore. I mean, after so many years of training it isn't like I needed a teacher, but he was a coach. A mentor. The closest thing I had to a friend. He understood me. My mother was with me nearly twenty-four hours a day, traveling with me, making sure I did what I had to do to keep the money coming in. To keep the spotlight on us. But she never really tried to know me."

Ethan moved to the piano, his palm flat on the glossy black surface. "It was her loss, Noelle."

Noelle's throat tightened. "You do know how to say some nice things, Ethan."

"It's a gift."

He looked down at her hand. "You still aren't wearing the ring."

"I don't... No. I can get it. It's the bathroom." Still in the box.

"You've got to put it on eventually. I'm planning an engagement party for us, you know. And we still don't look engaged."

She swallowed. "That won't work."

He leaned in and her breathing stalled. "No. It won't." He turned and walked from the room. Normally, the distance between them would let her breathe a bit easier, but not now. Because she knew what was coming next.

He returned with that blasted box in his hands, the one that had stayed closed since he first handed it to her on the boardwalk.

She stood up from the piano bench and locked her hands in front of her, trying to keep them from trembling. Trying to keep her expression neutral. It didn't mean anything. This was part of the show. The problem wasn't the ring, it was the importance she'd assigned to it. She just had to remember that it was just a prop.

He didn't get down on one knee, not that she'd thought he would, but she was relieved anyway. He held the box out, and this time, he opened it.

She could only stare at the ring, an antique platinum band with a large, square-cut diamond at the center. She didn't want to touch it. Didn't want to take the final step of putting it on her left hand. It was all well and good to say she was marrying him to get her house, but this made it so much more real. It forced her to face what she was doing.

"Wear my ring, Noelle?"

She lifted her hand, and there was no disguising the trembling in her fingers as she plucked the ring from its satin nest and slid it on. She made a fist, acutely aware of the thick band digging into the sides of her fingers.

"It's lovely," she said, trying to swallow around her heart, which seemed to have taken up permanent residence in her throat.

His Adam's apple bobbed and he took a step back. "It will be over soon."

She was supposed to feel relieved by that, but she didn't. She felt a little bit sick. "I know."

"I'll be pretty busy the rest of this week, but we'll get an engagement announcement in the paper. Party's on Friday."

She nodded. "Okay. I'll see you then." Five whole days without seeing Ethan. She should have felt relieved by that too. A chance to have space. A chance to get her thoughts in order.

But the stupid thing was, she missed him already.

CHAPTER NINE

It had been five days since he'd seen Noelle by the time the engagement party rolled around. Five days since she'd put his ring on her finger. It had been twenty-six days since he'd kissed her. Not that he was counting.

He shouldn't be counting anyway. Hard not to though, when just the thought of her was enough to tie him in knots. He couldn't remember ever wanting a woman more. Worse, he hadn't been able to force himself to look at another woman since the first day he'd seen Noelle.

It didn't change the fact that she was off limits. It was a joke, considering he had to hold and caress her like a lover for the entire evening.

He pulled Noelle closer as they walked into the hotel ballroom. He could feel her vibrating with energy beside him. Something in her was different, changed. She was alive. Not like the time they'd gone to see his grandparents, not like their first public appearance.

But then, this was about her.

He looked at her, at her broad smile and shining blue eyes. She was wearing red lipstick again, but this time, it made her glow with color, not appear more pale. It matched her scarlet dress, so bright against her alabaster skin, skimming her slender curves, flowing down over her body like a glimmering scarlet waterfall that caught the light with every step she took.

This party was about her. It was *for* her in a way. Everyone in the room was looking, and she was soaking it in like rays from the sun.

He recognized this, because it was what his mother had done. His mother, who was never satisfied, always needing more. Never getting enough from her family, from the ones who loved her. And there had been a time when it had become too much…when his father had twisted the knife too far.

He swallowed and tightened his hold on Noelle. He didn't think she would reach the lows his mother had. But the similarities were eerie enough. Strange that he'd initially been so determined to compare her with her mother, the woman who had caused so much pain in his life, and had ended up identifying her much more closely with his own.

"Noelle Birch!" Sylvie Ames, professional shopper and born socialite, approached them with a broad smile on her face.

He felt Noelle stiffen beside him. Going to Sylvie's party had been a pretty big source of stress for her, and he didn't know how she would feel actually having to talk to the woman.

"Sylvie," Noelle said, her voice soft, measured.

"I was wondering where you'd been, and now here you are, resurfaced with Mr. Ethan Grey. Now that's impressive! I was sorry I didn't get a chance to talk to you at my birthday party."

"Oh, I didn't mind. There were so many people."

"I always enjoyed your music. Do you have another album coming out soon? I'd love to have you play at a little soiree I'm planning for next month."

He felt Noelle relax beneath his hand as she exchanged dates and times and availability with Sylvie. Sylvie gave them both air kisses before sashaying away.

"Sounds like you have a gig," he said.

"I...yes," she said, sounding a little bit shocked. "I didn't think anyone would remember me."

"Why wouldn't they, Noelle? You've always been talented. You're bound to get more talented as time goes on, not less."

"It's not all talent, Ethan. It's about connections and marketability. A kid at a massive piano, barely able to reach the pedals, playing like an adult, people pay to see that. These days I've sort of outgrown my usefulness to the public."

"Who told you that?"

"No points for guessing, Ethan," she sighed, her voice resigned.

"Your mother. She's a right peach, Noelle. I think you should just assume everything she's ever told you is a load of crap. But that's just my thought on it."

"It's not that simple though. I really trusted her, all of my life. Didn't you trust your dad a little longer than you should have?"

He nodded, his lip curling at the thought of his old man. "I don't know. I don't know if I ever trusted him. But it was clear early on...he always spent more time with his mistresses than he did with us. I've lost count of how many times I saw a woman in a minidress leaving his office, still putting her shoes back on. I was young, but I wasn't stupid."

"Ethan, that's—"

He couldn't listen to an apology. Not from her. "It's nothing," he lied. "And once I have the resorts, there will be some justice. You can't just…treat people with such disregard and expect there to be no consequences."

Noelle offered a sparkling smile to a passing guest, one that rang false. "Well, that's what my mother's done. She took everything."

"She didn't take your talent."

"She took the music for a while."

"But it's back."

She frowned slightly. "It is. In some ways it's a bit more frightening than it being gone."

They were interrupted again by a line of well-wishers and fans of Noelle. The fact that her name was in the papers again seemed to have reminded everyone of who she was, of the fact that she had been out of the public eye for so long.

She did a good job glossing over the details of the past year. She claimed it had been a resting period. She was very like his mother in that way too. Able to hide failures beneath bright laughter and smooth little lies. On vacation. A hiatus. Suffering from exhaustion. Words his mother used instead of *no one will hire me* and *addicted to pills.*

But he didn't truly believe Noelle's career was over. She was beautiful and, without her nerves in play, she worked the crowd like magic. When she played it was like someone had reached into him and grabbed his heart, squeezing it tight.

She touched him with her music on a visceral level. And he couldn't be the only one. She had a gift, one that went beyond the novelty appeal of a small child at a big piano.

Ethan had no doubt she would regain that indefinable thing she needed to go on. The adoration of the crowd, her photo in the tabloids.

And he would have Grey's Resorts. A chance to watch his father's world broken into pieces, as Damien Grey had broken so many others. Maybe somewhere in that he would find some kind of satisfaction. Bloody perfect.

But those goals, goals that had obsessed him since he'd been a teenager, seemed strangely insignificant when he thought of his encounters with Noelle. And not just the moment in the hotel room, but the kiss on the boardwalk. Something so small, really. Something that wouldn't have mattered with any other woman.

The kiss was just a prelude, usually. It was never a main event in and of itself. Kissing Noelle was different. Suddenly, he wanted to kiss her more than he wanted his next breath.

Of course, the point of the party was to flaunt their relationship and promote their upcoming marriage, so maybe taking her into the garden to make out wouldn't be the most inappropriate thing.

He was strongly considering it when Sylvie approached them again, a much older man in tow. "Noelle, will you please play something? I know it's your party, but you're so amazing, and I was just telling Jacques how good you are. He's never had the pleasure of hearing you play live."

Jacques inclined his head. "I am a fan. It would be an honor."

Noelle looked at Ethan, her eyes bright with nerves and excitement. "Do you suppose the band would mind if I played something, just for a moment?"

Ethan shook his head, his body tight with frustration. "It's your party."

He watched as she wove through the crowd, a bright spot amid the sea of customary New York black. Golden hair, pale skin, silken red dress. She was a force of color and light that was impossible to ignore as she made her way to the stage.

And once she was there, sitting behind the piano, she commanded every eye in the room to watch her.

She put her hands on the piano and he swore he felt her fingertips on his body. Long, elegant fingers caressing the keys, easy to imagine them on his skin. She started playing a piece he recognized, one he'd heard in department stores many times. Something from one of her old albums, he assumed. But actually hearing it in person, watching her perform it, was a totally new experience.

It was so fluid. Smooth. Pure perfection.

And he felt as if it was only for him. Not for anyone else in the room. His chest tightened, breathing became a little harder as arousal assaulted him, flooded him.

Each note was a caress, the flow and rhythm of the song like making love, hard and fast then slow and sweet. Everything he wanted to do with her, everything he dreamed of, put out in the open, forcing him to confront it.

She lifted her head and looked into the crowd, looked at him. Her eyes locked with his as she continued to play, her entire body moving with the effort she put into playing, every part of her involved in her performance.

She would move like that in bed. Perfection. With passion, with all of herself.

He tightened his jaw, and the strain on his muscles was a welcome distraction from the desire that was pounding through him. The last thing he needed was for some photog to snap a picture of him sporting a hard-on over his fiancée's performance.

Of course, it would lend authenticity to the whole thing.

He frowned. He didn't like thinking of it that way. Didn't want to bring the agreement into this, because this was real. His desire for her felt more real than anything in his recent memory. His past affairs had all gone hazy thanks to the passage of time, but he truly didn't think he'd ever been so aroused by a woman who was more than a hundred feet away.

He wasn't the only one enthralled by her. Everyone was mesmerized, savoring every note, existing for the next. *Captive audience* didn't even begin to describe it

She had brought everyone in to her for a moment, let them all feel what was inside her. And, as the last note faded in the ballroom, the emotion lingered. At least it lingered in him. Everyone around him was applauding and he found that he couldn't. He wanted more. To hear more. To feel more.

But he couldn't have more. He wouldn't. Only this small indulgence. This window into her, into himself.

"She's amazing." This came from Jacques. The Frenchman was watching Noelle, his dark eyes shining, his mouth curved into a smile. Ethan wanted to hit him.

Unexpected and a little bit cavemanish. And yet, he was unrepentant.

"And she's mine," Ethan said, walking away from Sylvie and Jacques, weaving through the crowd and up to the stage, just in time to take Noelle's hand as she descended the steps.

"Was it okay?" she asked.

"Amazing." He bent his head and kissed her. Just part of the show. A necessary act that had no place lighting his body on fire.

When they parted, he was still having trouble breathing, his body tight with need.

"Amazing," she whispered.

"Let's hope this party ends soon," he said, his voice rough. Because he needed distance. He needed to send her back to her suite and he needed to get home to a very cold shower.

Walking away was the only option. But for the first time, he wondered if he had the strength to do it.

The kiss at the party had changed something. Or maybe it wasn't the kiss, maybe it was the performance. Or maybe it was both. Either way, the moment Ethan's lips had touched hers Noelle had made a decision.

She was going to have Ethan Grey. For a night, a few weeks, whatever, she was going to have what she wanted. With him.

Tonight she'd played. For her. And for everyone else. Without permission. And it had been amazing. The best feeling she could remember ever having on stage. It made her want more. Not just from Ethan, but from life. Why look ahead to the day she would get the house, shutting out everything else on the way? There was too much living to do between now and then.

She'd spent her whole life with tunnel vision. Play the piano. Be famous. Be brilliant. Everything else shut down and ignored.

But since meeting Ethan she'd discovered other things. Data entry and desire and a day at the beach. And she wanted more of that. Tonight, she was determined to have it.

Ethan stopped at the door of the hotel room. "I'll see you tomorrow."

"Wait." Good or bad, it was out of her mouth now. All she could do was commit and go forward. Or change the subject. Tell him he had lint on his coat? No. This wasn't the time to lose her nerve, or to worry about what he might think. It didn't matter. She couldn't be scared forever. And she wouldn't be scared now.

His eyes were nearly black in the shadow of the hall. "That might not be the best idea."

"I want to…play for you. The song I started in Australia. I want you to hear it."

He hesitated, his hands curled into fists, a muscle in his jaw shifting.

"Ethan…"

He took one step into the room. The tense lines in his body, the pronounced tendons in the backs of his hands, were proof of just how tightly he was hanging on to his control and told her that he knew what she was really asking.

And that by coming in, he hadn't committed to saying yes.

The risk of rejection was high. A little bit scary. But a lot worth it. Because Ethan did want her. And it was their connection, one that had nothing to do with the two of them but everything to do with their parents, that held him back. Maybe it should hold her back too. But she had never felt like her mother's actions, away from the cloistered life of music, had included her in any way.

She felt separate from their parents' history, separate in a way Ethan couldn't because of how it had affected his family. But maybe if he saw her, if he knew that she was nothing like her mother. Maybe then he would want to want her.

Ethan walked to the couch, his eyes trained on her as he worked the knot on his black silk tie. Her senses felt heightened. She could hear the slide of fabric over fabric as he tugged at it, could feel her heartbeat through her entire body. She could taste something in the air between them. Foreign and exciting. Tantalizing.

Maybe he had committed to her unspoken question. If it was even a question. It felt more like a command.

She moved to the piano, trying to imagine that there was a crowd, trying hard to hold on to her nerve. That crowd back at the party had been much easier to deal with. Even then she had felt Ethan watching her, had been compelled to turn and look at him. But it was easier to do with so many other people there. An audience of one was always much harder to perform for.

Because the more people there were, the more they blurred into an indistinguishable mass. When there were fewer of them, it suddenly became personal.

But rather than shutting Ethan out, she thought of just how he made her feel. She took a deep breath, put her hands on the keys and started playing. Slowly at first. She thought about ice cream and the beach. Ethan's hands on her body. His lips on hers. She didn't think about the future or about anything other than the immediate feelings Ethan gave her.

Lust, excitement. Happiness.

She shut everything out, everything except Ethan, and she played. Played for herself, to imprint the memories of what they'd shared inside her, to put it out there, the way some people would write in a diary. She wrote it into the song.

One she would be able to play whenever she wanted. Whenever she missed Ethan after all of this was done. Something to bring back the memories, clear and sharp, of what it had been like to be with him.

To simply share a conversation with him. A moment of pleasure.

Everything built to a crescendo, the rise of the music intense, exciting, mirroring how she felt now. The need for him. The fear he would say no. The fear he might say yes.

And then she stopped. It was quiet in the room, except for the sound of her uneven breathing. She took her shaking fingers from the keys and turned to him.

"That can't be the end," he said softly.

She shook her head and stood up, rounding the piano bench and moving towards the couch. "It's not. But I...I don't know how it ends. I was hoping you could show me."

The air was thick between them. Ethan sat unmoving, gripping the arm of the couch. She took another step toward him and his chest rose sharply, his fingers tightening their hold on the fabric.

"How do you want it to end, Noelle?" he asked, his voice tight, rough. Like each word took supreme effort to speak.

"I'd like to start where things left off that night in Australia. And I'd like them to end where they should have ended then."

"It should have ended before it started that night."

"But it didn't."

He swallowed, his Adam's apple dipping with the motion. "No. It didn't."

She took another step, stopping when she was right in front of him, her legs touching his. "So it's too late for that. We can ignore it, and neither of us is doing a great job of that, or we can see what it would be like. You and me."

She lifted her foot from the floor and rested her knee on the couch, next to his thigh. He lifted his hand and caught her wrist. "No matter what happens here, there will never be 'you and me.' I don't say that to hurt you, just to warn you. I'm not the kind of man who does forever. I don't even do long-term." He let go of her wrist and traced the line of her arm with his finger, up past her shoulder, the curve of her neck, along her jaw. He touched her lips, the contact soft. Erotic. "But what I do, I do well."

"That's all I'm asking from you, Ethan. Nothing more. I don't have any idea what I'm going to do when all of this is over, but that's not what I'm thinking about. Not now. For once I just want to…live. Right in the moment. To enjoy every last bit of now. To enjoy wanting you. The rest of it doesn't matter. Not right now."

She lifted her other foot off the floor, resting her knee beside his other thigh. He curved his arm around her body and placed his hand on her lower back, the heat of his flesh through her thin silk dress warming her, spreading sweet heat through her body, pooling in her belly, flowing out to her limbs, making them feel heavy.

He captured her mouth with his, their breathing mixing together, harsh and uneven. He slid his other hand down her thigh, gripping the skirt of her dress and tugging it upward, pushing slick silk up around her hips.

His hand met the bare skin of her buttocks. She'd gone with the filmy-fabric-friendly option of a thong when she'd dressed tonight. She was glad she had now. Even more so when a harsh groan escaped his lips and he squeezed her gently.

She gasped when he dipped his finger beneath her underwear, teasing her lightly, sliding over damp flesh.

He pulled his lips away from hers, pressed them to her neck. "How do you want this?" he asked. "I want you to set the tempo. Show me what you like. Show me how you think the song ends."

She put her hands on his shoulders and tilted her hips, a sharp whimper escaping her lips when the movement pushed his fingers forward, the tips grazing the sensitive bundle of nerves at the apex of her thighs.

"Good," he said, his voice hoarse.

She repeated the motion, pleasure streaking through her like fire. She tilted her head down and rested it on his shoulder as she continued to move over his hand. He dipped one finger inside her and all the tension that had been building in her broke, unraveling, spiraling through her in waves of sweet satisfaction, so acute it was almost painful.

She leaned against him, her entire body limp, weak. Her dress was clinging to her damp skin, her hair sticking to her neck. And he didn't seem to mind. He wrapped his arms around her and held her on his lap, his lips by her ear.

"I wondered if you would be as passionate about making love as you are about playing the piano. I think that question was just answered."

"For me too," she said softly. "I had no idea…"

He kissed her again, his mouth hungry, devouring. And she felt an answering hunger in her own body, arousal building even faster than before. Now she knew what he could make her feel, knew how powerful it was, how amazing it felt. And she knew he could make her feel that way again.

He put his hand on her bottom and stood, supporting her weight with one arm. She locked her legs around his lean hips, the hard length of his erection pressed against her clitoris. Every step he took sent waves of bliss through her, renewed her need for him.

He pushed open the door to her bedroom and walked to the bed, bringing them both gently down onto the mattress, his body covering hers. She arched against him, pressing her breasts against his chest. He reached around and unzipped her dress, tugging it down, baring her breasts. His eyes glittered in the dim light of the bedroom.

"You're even more beautiful than I remembered. And I didn't think that was possible. I thought for sure I must have imagined that you were this perfect."

Her throat tightened, emotion building in her. Emotion she didn't want to deal with. Not now. Not when she simply wanted to live in this glorious moment.

"I remember you being pretty perfect too," she said, ignoring the persistent ache in chest. "You might want to refresh my memory."

He pushed himself up with one arm and shrugged his jacket off, pulling his undone tie over his shoulders and casting it to the floor. She watched, every bit of her completely enthralled, as he unbuttoned his white dress shirt, revealing teasing glimpses of perfect, muscular chest and abs that had not come to him by accident.

He let the shirt fall from his body and started working at his belt. Her mouth went cotton-dry, her eyes fixed on him. She didn't want to miss anything, not one second. This was her moment—their moment—and she was savoring it.

Ethan let his belt fall open and undid the fastening on his slacks, tugging his pants and underwear off in one fluid motion.

She rose up onto her knees, letting her dress fall around her body. She'd expected to feel nervous or unsure, but she didn't, she knew just what she wanted. She moved forward and gripped his erection, the flesh hot and smooth, different than she'd imagined. When she squeezed him, his head fell back, a raw sound of satisfaction rushing from him.

She leaned in and flicked her tongue over the head of his shaft, a sharp sensation of desire and power racing through her when he reached out to grab her shoulder, like he needed something to brace himself against, as she had earlier.

"You want me," she said, feeling a little bit shocked by the revelation. Not just that he wanted her in a vague, sexual sense, but that he wanted her in the way she wanted him. In that knees-buckling, body-shaking sort of way.

"More than my next breath," he panted.

He moved back onto the bed, his hands moving over her curves as he bent her backward. She stretched out beneath him as he cupped her breast, his thumb skimming her nipple. He dipped his head and tasted her, pulling the hardened tip between his lips.

She arched, her hips lifting from the bed, and he took advantage, tugging her thong down her legs. She kicked it off the rest of the way, not feeling even a moment's embarrassment over being naked with him. There was no room for embarrassment. There wasn't room for anything other than the fierce need she felt to have more of him.

To feel the rush of orgasm with his body joined to hers. To give him the kind of pleasure he'd already given her.

He reached over to the side table and fumbled around for a moment before pulling out a condom. "Oh good," he said. "I don't have to fire anyone today."

"Don't tell me you knew this would happen."

"No. But my suites are always supposed to be stocked with basic amenities."

"You really are all about full service."

He smiled and pressed a kiss to her neck, then nipped her lightly, immediately following it up with a pass of his tongue. "I told you I was all about service." He moved his hand down in between her thighs, stroking her, heightening her arousal.

"I believe it," she whispered.

"Ready?" He tore the condom packet open and rolled the protection onto his length quickly before moving back over her.

"I've been ready for a long time," she said. She put her hands on his shoulders, held onto him as he pushed into her.

It didn't hurt, not in the dramatic way it seemed to in some of the books she'd read. But she was thankful tha he went slowly, that he gave her a chance to adjust to him, time to savor her first moments of full intimacy with him.

He flexed his hips and buried himself to the hilt, his muscles locking in place, his breath coming out in harsh, short bursts. "Are you all right?"

"Great," she replied. "I'm great."

He looked at her, and for a moment she saw darkness in his eyes, a sadness that stole the air from her lungs. She put her hand on his cheeks and kissed his lips.

"Please, Ethan," she said.

His answer was the short thrust of his hips, a movement that sent a sharp burst of pleasure through her. He moved in her, building her desire, low and intense in her pelvis, deeper than the first time. Stronger, which she hadn't even imagined possible.

She could feel his control slipping, as each movement became less measured, less controlled. All of that will-power he carried like a millstone around his neck seemed to fall away, leaving only the man, without his civility, without the trappings of modern society.

Now, in this moment, he was simply a man, and she was a woman—his woman. And she reveled in it, moving with him, against him. She felt she was drowning, not just in pleasure, in emotion. In the connection she felt with him. As if he was truly a part of her.

She felt whole, and she felt herself splintering into pieces at the same time, her orgasm rushing up, tangling with the tide of emotion that was crashing inside of her. Ethan stiffened above her, her name on his lips as he found his own release.

This time, it was her turn to hold him, his head resting on her chest, his breath cool on her sweat-slicked skin. Silence filled the room, but it wasn't awkward. It made the air feel close, like it was holding them together. Keeping them cocooned, shielded from reality. At least for now.

She ran her fingers through his hair. She didn't think she could ever get enough—not just of the amazing things he made her feel, but of what it was like simply to have him in her arms. To be in his.

She didn't know how long they lay there. But finally Ethan sat up. "I should go take care of some things."

He got out of bed and went into the bathroom, returning a few moments later and sliding back in beside her. He pulled her to him, his arms encircling her.

"I don't know if there's any music that can capture this," she said, moving her fingertips over his chest.

"If anyone could write it, you could," he said. "You told me earlier that it wasn't my business who you've slept with, and if you still feel that way, that's fine. But I'm going to ask anyway."

"I'll save you the trouble. No lovers. None besides music. Isn't that a dramatic way to put it?"

"I don't want to hurt you, Noelle."

"Then don't."

"It's not that simple."

"It can be. We'll stick to the deal. We can have this, whatever it is, and then…and then we'll both walk away with what we want. That's simple right?" Even as she spoke the words, she knew they weren't true.

"Sounds good." And she could tell by his answer he knew it too.

Ethan just held Noelle, not even tempted to slip out of the room and head back to his condo. In fact, that idea was the opposite of appealing. Strange, since he was usually ready to do a runner by this point.

But Noelle was different. And not in the way men said

women were different when they just wanted to get into their knickers. Different in a real, profound way. And not just because she'd been a virgin.

He was her first lover. That…well, that meant something. At thirty he was well past the age where he expected to run across a virgin. He'd even avoided them in high school, mostly by choosing to have sex with older women. He'd never really fancied the idea of being a corruptor of innocents. His life was just too…raw. He'd never had true innocence himself.

It was impossible when the cupboards in his kitchen had more prescription pills than they did food. Impossible when he overheard loud fights and sex between his parents every other day. Impossible when he simply felt invisible in his own home.

His upbringing had been privileged financially, but bankrupt in every other way.

But what had just happened between him and Noelle hadn't seemed corrupt at all. Far from it. It had been the best sex of his life. And it had meant something. Had altered something in him.

He wasn't sure if he liked that, but it was the truth.

It wouldn't last. A fact that made his chest feel like it was filled with tiny shards of glass, evil and sharp, impossible to remove.

It couldn't last. That was the one thing he was certain of. Because she would never be happy with him. His stomach suddenly felt too tight. It was very hard to breathe. It was a hard admission to make, but it was true.

He'd never managed to bring happiness to anyone in his life. There was no reason Noelle would be any different.

He would never be able to make her happy, not in the long term. He would ruin her.

No. That wouldn't happen. He wouldn't do that to her. They would have their affair, and they would both move on.

Even if there was a small, insidious part of himself that wished things could be different. They couldn't be. And he would have to accept it.

CHAPTER TEN

NOELLE stretched, smiling when she felt a couple little aches in some very intimate places. Oh yes, Ethan had been amazing. Over and over again.

She had been well and truly introduced to sex.

Her smiled faded a little as she recognized a new ache, right around her heart. She was also being introduced to something else, something big and new. Emotions, a connection she'd never felt with anyone before.

She didn't know what to call it. Or maybe she was too scared to call it anything.

Ethan saw her. More than that, he *wanted* to see her. Who she really was, not the veneer. No one, not her mother, not her piano teacher, not the flighty acquaintances who had sometimes called themselves her friends had ever bothered to do that.

"Good morning." Ethan came into the bedroom holding a tray with coffee and muffins. He wasn't wearing much more than a smile, his broad chest bare, powerful thighs on display. Only a very brief pair of briefs covered him. She wished he hadn't put them on.

"You are every woman's fantasy," she smiled, sitting up.

"In my spare time." He sat on the bed with her, raising a mug of hot coffee to his lips, his eyes trained on her. "You're most definitely my fantasy."

"I probably have makeup smeared down my face."

"There's a certain debauched charm in that look."

"Yeah, I bet."

"You got a call."

"I did?"

"Yes, Jacques D'ambois left a message on my phone for you."

"The man that was at the engagement thing with Sylvie last night?"

"The same."

She frowned and took a bite of chocolate muffin. "I wonder what he wants."

"If he wants to seduce you, tell him he's about twelve hours too late." Ethan said it as a joke, but there was a hint of seriousness in his words.

"No worries there, Ethan. I'll call him after breakfast. And I'll be sure to let him know I'm no longer in need of seducing."

"Now that the big engagement party is out of the way, we need to move on to the planning of the actual wedding."

"Oh yes, that." Her heart sank a little. Now it seemed… it seemed much more complicated, this whole wedding thing.

"Don't look like that, Noelle. This," he indicated the bed, "has to stay separate from the business arrangement we have. The wedding is still a business arrangement."

"No, no, I know! I just…well, all right, it seems a bit more personal now, I can't lie. But I get it, Ethan, I do. I don't want a real marriage anyway." Did she? She didn't think she did. Marriage was….well, her mother had never been married to her father. And it seemed that to Ethan's father, marriage vows had been merely a suggestion. A suggestion he hadn't taken. What was the point of it?

"You don't?"

"No. Not now. Maybe someday."

"Marriage is a crock anyway."

"You think so?"

"What is it, really, Noelle? So, we're getting married. And what do we have to do to get married? Love each other? Make vows we'll keep? No. We just have to sign a legal form. Marriage never made my parents happy. It gave them both a new kind of status, and that was the point for them. My mother was able to spend my father's money, my father had a beautiful trophy wife who walked red carpets and had her name up in lights. Until she didn't, of course. And then he cared a lot less for her. Which was when he started finding other women."

"That's...well, that's bad." Noelle looked down at her coffee. "Love is real though," she said softly. "Isn't it?" She wanted to believe it was. That maybe someday... She ignored the sudden, deep tightening in her stomach, a kind of grief at the thought of a future without Ethan.

Ethan stared at a point beyond her. "I think so. I think it's pretty sadistic though, to be honest with you. I think my mother loves my father, still, in spite of all he's done to her. I think my father loved your mother. Even though he was married to mine. When my mother stopped getting invited to Hollywood events, he stopped bothering to take her out in public. That was when he started going with Celine Birch. When he let the world know he didn't care enough for my mother to even try and shield her from his affair."

Ethan's lips curled. "I remember there was this big premiere my mother was desperate to go to, and your mother got invited. The next day it was all over the tabloids how Celine and my father had been all over each other."

"Oh. That's awful."

"There's more. There's a reason I can't…there's a reason I have to do this, Noelle." He still didn't look at her, his expression fixed, his dark eyes blank. "I came home from school that day, and, of course, all the kids had already seen the news. They were taunting me. And when I came home it was so quiet. The television wasn't on, and she always had it on. I went to look for her. She was face down on the bathroom floor. I was fifteen, but I had learned some CPR in school. Thankfully the ambulance came quickly, because my skills weren't really up to the task. It was the paramedics who found her pills. They were the ones who figured out she'd done it to herself."

"Oh, Ethan…"

"That's love, Noelle. That's what it does. It's one person trying and trying and never being able to be enough. I don't want to be a part of it. And I sure as hell can't let my father come out of it unscathed."

Sickness weighed her down, enveloped her being. "I can't believe they were both so selfish…I can't believe…"

"It was a long time ago. And I'm not seeking any kind of sympathy. But now you understand why I feel the way I do, not just about love, but about my father getting his hands on Grey's."

"I understand."

He was silent then and she knew he was done talking about his mother.

"So, the wedding, when is it?" she asked.

"I thought we might keep it low-key. Elope even. At this point, the scale of the wedding doesn't matter. Only that there is one."

"That's…good." A rush of relief flooded her. She didn't

want to do the white and the cathedral and the priest. Elvis and the Vegas strip would be much more appropriate. It would be easier. It wouldn't be so likely to trick her raw emotions into thinking it was anything more than what it was.

"Great. I'll see about arranging all the legalities."

She blew out a breath. "And they say romance is dead."

Ethan looked at her, his dark eyes blazing. "I'll show you romance, Noelle. It'll just be separate from this."

He turned and walked out of the room and she couldn't help but watch his butt, barely covered by skin-tight black briefs. He was so hot. And what they had might not be the epitome of love and flowers but it made her feel alive.

More alive than she'd ever felt.

That had to count for something. That had to make it worth it. Whatever it was.

"Keep telling yourself that," she said into the empty room.

She could angst about Ethan later. For now, she would get dressed and give Jacques a call.

An audition. She had an audition.

Auditions are beneath her. She's Noelle Birch.

Her mother's words rang in her head. Words that seemed meaningless when she hadn't had a job in forever. Auditions most certainly weren't beneath her. That attitude, fuelled not by snobbery but by a genuine desire to avoid the public discovering that she was a falling star rather than a rising one, was what had kept her down for the past year.

She was over it now. Over just sitting around and letting life happen to her.

Ethan walked into the large sitting area of the penthouse. He was wearing black slacks and a white button-up shirt, open at the collar. His hair was wet from the shower. He looked delicious. And all she wanted to do was take that perfectly tailored outfit off of his body so she could taste all of his fresh clean skin.

"Busy this weekend?" he asked.

Not busy until next weekend. "This weekend? As in... tomorrow? No." She lifted her coffee cup to her lips and tried to look casual. She didn't want to tell him about the audition. It was too new. And what if she screwed it up? What if Jacques ended up not wanting her to play either?

"Good. We're getting married."

She snorted into the hot liquid and it sloshed over the side of the cup. "A little warning please."

"I told you I was going to arrange it. I think after the engagement party it will be romantic if we simply elope, don't you?"

"You mean less of a hassle for us?"

"Yes, that's exactly what I mean, but I'm spinning the headline."

"Right."

"We just have to get through this part, Noelle. A few weeks of marriage, a few signed papers. And then you're free. I'm free. We'll both have what we want."

Money. The audition. A chance at starting over, at grasping the fame she used to have. The luxury. She'd thought she'd find that with Ethan, and she had.

It didn't really make her happy though, and she wasn't sure why. She didn't want to think about why.

"Great. Yes. Yay for met goals and all of that."

"When I put my mind to something, it gets done."

"Yeah, I uh...remember that. From last night." She felt her face get hot and she cursed her pale skin, knowing she was wearing her embarrassment like a neon sign.

* * *

Ethan's stomach tightened. Noclle's face was flushed and she looked perfect. Perfect to take to bed and spend hours kissing, tasting, making love to. But he couldn't afford that. He couldn't afford the strange kind of attachment he felt for her.

He'd made the decision sometime during his shower as he'd dealt with a hard-on that refused to quit. She was sexy, no doubt. Compelling and amazing in bed. But he didn't have time for a lover, especially not a lover who had such a strong effect on him. Not after Grey's was signed over to him.

This relationship was on a very tight timetable. As soon as the ink hit the signature line on the divorce decree, that was the end. Because a new contract would take priority then, and Noelle...well, she would be taken care of, at least. He would make sure of that.

He breathed in deeply, trying to loosen the feeling in his gut. It felt as if someone had reached a hand inside of him and grabbed his stomach in their fist.

"I would love to push you back against the wall right now and go in for some hard and fast," he said, arousal and the general direction of his thoughts making his voice rough. "But I think you might need some recovery time. And we have a plane to catch."

Noelle looked uncomfortable with his choice of words, and he didn't really blame her. He was being an ass because he wanted her, and he was contemplating never having her again at the same time his body throbbed with need of her.

"A plane?" she asked, pale eyebrows arched.

"Oh yeah, we really are getting married in Vegas."

"Are you kidding me?"

"No. How tacky would you like it?"

He was rewarded with a smile. Maybe, just maybe things could get back on good footing. Maybe they could have the next month together. Sating their desire for each other, and hanging out as companions. Because whether they were in bed or not, he simply liked having her around.

Bloody hell, that was complicated.

"Maybe not Elvis-tacky, but I feel like a leopard-print wedding dress might be pretty awesome."

"Are you joking?"

She rolled her eyes. "Well, I can't wear white, Ethan, and don't pretend you don't know why. You were there last night."

"I'll never forget it." That part he said with absolute sincerity. Because he knew for a fact that he would never forget Noelle.

He knew it with a certainty he couldn't recall ever feeling before. No matter how many women came after her, no matter how much time passed, the memory of her silken skin beneath his fingertips would linger. And it would always make him burn.

He wondered if she would think of him like that. Or if he would fade in her mind. That seemed to be the way most people felt about him.

He closed off that train of thought, tried to get his breathing steady.

"Right. Well, I guess we both need to pack."

Their quick flight to Las Vegas had already appeared on some entertainment news websites by the time Ethan's private plane had touched down in Nevada. Speculation about a wedding was already rampant, of course, because in Vegas, gambling or a quickie wedding was usually on the docket.

Either way, it was newsworthy.

Noelle looked pale, her blue eyes large in her face as he took out the keycard to the hotel suite and unlocked the door. They were staying in one of Grey's most famous resorts, a den of sin and sex that was infamous even on the strip, adding to the irony of his grandfather's insistence on him marrying, being a family man before he took over the company.

"You all right?" Ethan asked.

Noelle looked up from the smartphone. "Just reeling. The speculation is intense. Frighteningly accurate."

He took the phone out of her hands. "In what way?"

"Just that we came here to get married."

"Nothing about a leopard-print wedding dress?"

She laughed, a high, kind of unnatural sound. "Uh, no."

He took her hand in his, her skin so soft and tempting it made him ache. "Are you okay, really?"

"Do I look that bad?"

"You look nervous."

"We're getting married tomorrow. And I know it's not *married* married, and I know it shouldn't matter. But it's kind of overwhelming."

He wanted to kiss her. But he also felt as if resisting the impulse was important. He needed to get a grip on this… thing between them. Not that he wasn't going to sleep with her again. He planned on it. But he needed to be in control. To rid himself of that shaky, wild feeling that overtook him when her tongue touched his.

That sensation of being a teenage virgin that he couldn't quite seem to shake. Well, he *was* shaking it.

He pushed open the door to the hotel suite.

"Wow," Noelle said, walking into the room, her eyes fixed on the crystal chandelier hanging low in the center of the massive entryway. "This is…"

"You said you wanted tacky."

"Eek."

She walked over to the transparent bar, built from thick

Plexiglas and fashioned into a kind of art-deco piece that seemed to transcend style. And taste. The walls were glossy too, and they seemed to be made from some kind of opaque, frosted glass. It was all extremely expensive, from the plush carpets to the rich drapes, it was just lacking in any kind of restraint.

"This place makes a killing," he said. "Just so you know."

"Well, it is kind of fun. And hey, why not? It goes with the fake wedding."

"We could have the reception here," he suggested dryly.

"Oh no, please tell me we're not really having a reception."

"No. That's the point of eloping."

"You're right. Let's do it now."

"Now?"

"Yes." She looked determined, a glint in her blue eyes. Startling and arousing. "Marry me now. Why wait until tomorrow? There are twenty-four-hour chapels and very loose laws about obtaining licenses in this state, and I say we make the most of it."

"You seem to know a lot about it. Is there anything you need to tell me?"

"No quickie marriages in my past, but time spent playing the Vegas Strip? Oh yeah. I did shows here for a year when I was nine."

"You're sort of amazing, do you know that?" he asked.

Her cheeks darkened. "I never really thought so, but, thank you."

"I say we go find a chapel," he said.

The sooner they got the marriage out of the way, the sooner everything could be finished. All the loose ends tied up. All the paperwork signed. Grey's Resorts moved into his name. And he would have the satisfaction of see-

ing his father's face as he confronted him with everything
he would never have.

So why was the wedding night all he could think about?

CHAPTER ELEVEN

ETHAN wore jeans and a tight black T-shirt. And Noelle had managed to find a leopard-print skirt and black tank top in the gift shop on their way to the nearest chapel.

The car ride was silent until they pulled in to the parking lot. The white chapel, framed with neon lighting, was like a beacon amongst all the color of the strip. Bold letters boasted they had low waits and good rates.

Noelle snickered. All of it was simply too absurd, too wondrously insane not to be enjoyed.

"What?" Ethan asked.

"This is the funniest, craziest thing I've ever done."

"Ranks up there for me too."

He got out of the limo and rounded the shiny black beast of a car, opening her door for her.

"Such a gentleman," she said. "No wonder I said yes."

"And I'm paying you a lot of money."

Her stomach tightened. "Yeah. And that." She didn't want a reminder of that. Not now.

She followed him through the double doors and into the little building. It was much more sedate than its exterior implied.

"You're Noelle Birch!" The girl standing behind the counter, her hair dyed blue-black and cropped short, her arms decorated with tattoos, looked at Noelle with wide eyes.

"Uh…yes. I am."

"Wow. I have all your CDs. I begged my mom to let me take piano lessons because of you."

"Oh…wow. That's…a really great compliment. Thank you."

"I kind of suck. I mean, I don't suck, but I play here for weddings, so how good can I be, right?"

Noelle looked over at Ethan, then back at her fan. "I don't play much of anywhere anymore myself."

"Getting married though, huh?"

"Yes. Yes I am."

"We'll take the paperwork," Ethan said.

"Right!" The girl bent down behind the counter and popped back up with a clipboard. "Just sign and date. Do you want Elvis? He's extra."

"No," she and Ethan answered in unison.

"Somehow, I didn't figure you would. I'm Tara, by the way."

"Hi, Tara. Nice to meet you," Noelle said.

"Thanks."

Noelle exchanged an awkward smile with Tara while Ethan quickly filled the form out before passing it to her. Her fingers shook as she gripped the pen, and her writing reflected that.

She signed it and Ethan added a check to the papers before passing it back.

"Sweet. That's one way to get your autograph," Tara said.

"I could…sign something…else."

Tara produced a blank sheet of paper and Noelle signed it while Ethan stood next to her, his impatience apparent.

"We'll just take the next available officiant," Ethan said. "If he happens to be Elvis I'm all right with that."

"Nah, I think Janine is free. Just a sec."

Tara disappeared behind a purple curtain and Noelle looked over at Ethan. "You were the one who wanted to get married in Vegas," she said.

"I wanted no fuss."

"This is no fuss. There aren't five hundred people here, are there?"

"No."

"Will your grandparents be upset that they weren't invited?"

He frowned. "It's better they aren't here. I don't really want them getting too attached to this. To us."

She tried to ignore the sharp stab of hurt his comment left behind. He'd said the wedding was separate from their personal stuff. So she shouldn't go getting weepy and hurt now.

"No. No of course not," she said quickly.

Tara appeared again, a smile on her face as she rounded the counter. "This way." She gestured to a long hallway and led them through the second door. "I'd ask if you wanted to pay for a pianist but…I'm pretty sure you don't want to hear me play. We have one of your CDs here though. I'll put it on. And congratulations!"

Ethan looked up at the domed ceiling and Noelle followed his gaze. There was a poor reproduction of the Sistine Chapel's mural painted there.

"This is depressing," Ethan said.

Music floated in over the speakers. Very familiar music. "Not as depressing as that," Noelle frowned.

"It's nice."

"Thanks, Ethan." She smiled as the familiar notes continued. "It's funny because when I'm nervous I go over pieces in my head, imagine how I play them. Fast. Slow. Soft. Loud. It helps get me focused. Now my music is playing for me."

"Have you done that since I've known you?"

"Yes. Lots."

"I make you nervous?"

"Sometimes. Mostly you just make me excited," she admitted, the words spilling out in a rush.

He studied her face, his dark eyes filled with intensity. "Noelle…"

A woman with a very similar look to Tara walked in, Tara trailing behind, acting as a witness. "Hi there, you must be Ethan and Noelle. Are you ready to do this?"

Noelle looked at Ethan again and her heart slammed against her breastbone. She was ready. And that was scary. Because here they were in the world's tackiest place to get married. Ethan looked like he was headed to the gallows and they had an officiant with a nose ring. And yet, it felt right.

If it had been a huge wedding with a big white gown and a harpist, she might expect that. Might expect to be lured in by the fantasy. But there was no fantasy here. Only a stained green carpet and fake flowers woven through tacky white lattice.

And it felt momentous. And amazing. And it shouldn't.

Janine gave the most informal, straightforward version of marriage vows Noelle had ever heard. Nothing florid or personal, just the legal stuff.

"Do you have rings?" Janine asked.

"Oh…" Noelle felt stupid for wishing she had a ring for Ethan. The wedding didn't mean anything, and a ring would mean even less. But for some reason, the image of a thin gold band on Ethan's left hand made her feel short of breath.

"I do." Ethan reached into his pocket and took out a small box. He opened it slowly, the glitter of the large center stone catching in the overhead lighting.

"Ethan…"

He took her hand in his and pulled the ring from its silken nest, sliding it gently onto her finger. "A woman as unique and special as you deserves something equally special."

It was both of those things. A band that was shaped to fit her unique engagement ring, diamonds encircling the platinum, the precious metal fashioned into vines, the stone like glittering flowers.

"I don't know…I didn't know." This was a ring beyond her expectation or imagination.

It locked together perfectly with the engagement ring. A perfect set. A perfect couple. Unlike them.

"And now, by the power vested in me by the State of Nevada, I pronounce you husband and wife. You can kiss now," Janine said.

Ethan didn't hesitate. And for that she was grateful. He pulled her into his arms, his kiss starving, devouring. And she was right there with him. She was dizzy with her desire for him, with the need to do so much more than kiss him. She hadn't realized just how much a day without physical contact had worn on her.

He slowed the kiss down, the movements of his mouth less ravenous but still deep, his tongue stroking over hers. When he started to move away, he paused, pressing another kiss to the side of her lips, then the other side.

She really did melt then, his strong arms the only thing keeping her from sliding to the floor.

"Wow," she breathed.

Then Ethan laughed, a smile curving those talented lips of his. "Glad you feel that way."

Janine fanned herself with her notes. "I'm with her. Wow."

"You're universally appreciated," Noelle smiled at Ethan.

Ethan forced a tight smile in return. "Is that it?"

"Yes. You're married. Mr. and Mrs...." she checked her notes, "Grey."

"All right then." Ethan took her hand in his. "Thank you."

"Don't forget your marriage license." She handed Ethan the documents they'd signed earlier, which now boasted both Janine's and Tara's signatures too. "All legal now."

Ethan took the license from Janine and folded it carefully. It was done. The marriage was legal. It was the last thing he needed to get his grandfather to sign the resorts over to him. But he didn't feel particularly accomplished. His long-range goal seemed hazy, blotted out by the desire that was pounding through him.

He'd expected a few hours to give him dominion over the need he felt for Noelle, but it didn't seem to be working that way.

It'll burn out. You know it will. It always does.

Lust was like that. Hot and bright at first, but it burned out quickly. There was no real fuel to sustain the blaze. Just a brilliant flash, spectacular for a moment, then growing cold after that first real explosion.

This was lasting a bit longer. Probably because Noelle had been a virgin. And because he'd spent so much time with her. He genuinely liked her, felt a connection with her. But that seemed natural. Normal, really.

Not that anything about the pure, liquid desire rushing through his veins seemed natural or normal.

Later. After tonight. After he made love to Noelle, he would call his grandfather to get the ball rolling on the acquisition of Grey's. Until then though, he had to clear his thoughts. And he didn't think he'd even be able to see straight if he didn't have Noelle as soon as possible.

"We need to get on with the wedding night," he whispered, his voice rough. "As soon as possible."

Her cheeks turned deep pink again and he felt an ache that started in his stomach and spread low to his groin. He wanted her so much it was beyond his experience. Again, she unmanned him. Made *him* feel like the virgin.

He didn't know how she managed to do that.

"I'm all for that," she whispered back.

"Not playing Mozart in your head, are you?"

"No. When I'm with you now it just kind of…flows. I hear music all the time."

He ignored the tightening in his chest and focused on that in his pants. It was safer. A bit more familiar.

"Come on."

He led her out of the chapel and back into the warm, dry evening. The limo was still there, idling in front of the chapel. He opened the door for her, she slid inside, and he joined her. As soon as the door was closed he pulled her into his arms, kissing her, tasting her, trying to sate the deep, gnawing hunger that seemed ever-present in him. A hunger that he didn't know if he could satisfy.

He could lose himself trying. And that didn't seem like such a bad prospect.

He couldn't remember the last time kissing had felt like the main event. Maybe the last time he'd kissed Noelle. Usually, at this point, he'd be undressing one of them, but at the moment, he simply wanted to taste her. Savor her.

To run his hands over her curves, delight in the fact that there was more to come. Sweeter. Sexier. Smoother. Drawing it out was heightening his pleasure in ways he'd never imagined it could.

He was so lost in the simple act of kissing her that he

didn't know the limo had pulled back up to the hotel until she pulled away from him.

"We're here."

"Yeah. Damn. I'm tempted to ask the driver to drive around the block a few times."

"A bed would be a decent idea," she said softly.

"One day though, we'll have to give the limo a go."

"Promise."

He opened the door and took her hand, drawing her out with him to the neon-lit entryway of the hotel. He watched as the colors alternated, white and red, casting different hues over her pale features.

"You really do belong in the spotlight," he said, his throat tight.

"I don't want the spotlight just now," she said, running her hands down his arms, the gesture innocuous but, in that moment, with her, enough to make his knees want to buckle.

"I don't either."

He took her hand in his again and walked quickly through the lobby, not caring if people stared, or if they knew just where they were going and what they were going to do.

Nothing mattered but Noelle. Having her. Being with her. Being in her.

During the elevator ride he was tempted to just hit the stop button and finish it there. But he wanted more than that. Longer than that. He wanted all night. To take her to bed and not get back up for at least twelve hours.

That sounded close to heaven.

When the elevator doors opened they moved across the hall to their suite door. His hands shook as he pushed the card into the lock.

He closed the door and she leaned against it, a slight smile on her lips.

"Noelle," he said. It was the only word he could think to say. It was the only word in his mind.

She kept her eyes locked with his, so sincere. So beautiful. She gripped the hem of her black tank top and pulled it over her head, revealing a simple black bra that shouldn't be anywhere near as sexy as it was. But it was hotter than any French lingerie he'd ever seen.

"I've never seen a more beautiful woman. And I mean that," he said.

"I've never seen a more beautiful man," she replied. "Return the favor already."

She didn't have to ask twice. He pulled his T-shirt over his head, gratified that she was affected by the sight of his body. Her breathing was more labored now, her cleavage rising and falling sharply.

"Your turn," he said.

She smiled and pushed that ridiculous leopard skirt down her hips, shimmying slightly as she worked the tight fabric over her curves. She was wearing a black…oh, he hoped it was a thong…that matched her bra.

"Your turn," she repeated.

He reached for the snap on his jeans, lowered the zip, his eyes on hers. They were round and riveted on his body. She didn't even try to hide her interest. Her reactions were honest, her desire for him easily seen.

It only made him hotter. Harder.

He shrugged his jeans down, along with his underwear, and kicked them to the side. The look on Noelle's face was enough to finish him then and there. She looked…fascinated, and hungry at the same time and it was doing things to him that he couldn't put a name to.

He closed the distance between them and locked his hands around her wrists, drawing her arms up over her head, against the door, as he pressed his chest against her breasts and kissed her. She arched against him, her hip brushing his erection.

He let out a rough groan and deepened the kiss, sliding his tongue against hers, reveling in the slick friction.

She wiggled against him. "Let me go."

"Why?" he kissed her shoulder.

"So I can undo my bra."

He licked the curve of her neck and blew against it, taking deep, masculine satisfaction in her shivered response. "I can do that." He used his free hand to snap the clasp open on her bra, letting it fall loose.

"It can't come off if you keep holding me prisoner."

"But I can work with this." He pushed the silky material up and revealed her breasts. He cupped her, sliding his thumb over her nipple. "Oh yeah, I can work with this."

She arched against him. "Ethan."

"What?"

"More. I can't wait."

"Patience is a virtue."

"I don't want to be patient."

"I've been patient," he said, lowering his head and flicking the tip of his tongue over her nipple. "I've been patient all day. It won't hurt you to wait."

She sucked in a sharp breath. "I think it will."

"I won't hurt you. I promise." He meant physically. He wished he could promise it in a deeper way. That he could swear he would slay her dragons and make everything better. But he was no white knight. Come to that, Noelle wasn't a princess locked in a tower. She was a woman. One who could take care of herself.

And that was something he found comfort in. Because God knew he wasn't up to the task.

He ignored the fierce tearing sensation in his chest and focused instead on her body. On touching her. Loving her. This was the way he knew how to do it. The best he could give. And he would give it all.

He abandoned her breasts and tugged her panties down her legs, sliding his fingers through the pale curls at the apex of her thighs, rubbing her moisture over her clitoris.

"Ethan…" His name was a plea on her lips and he couldn't get enough.

His whole body was hard, tense, needy. But he needed to give to her first. Needed her to take every last bit of pleasure that she could. He needed to give it to her.

Her lips parted, her head moving back and forth as he stroked her. She arched her body against his again, pressing herself more firmly against his hand. He penetrated her slowly with one finger and felt her tighten around him, a short sound of pleasure escaping her lips.

He let her ride out her orgasm and then slowly released his hold on her wrists. She slumped down the wall an inch, her breathing coming out in short, sharp gasps.

She moved and let her bra fall to the floor, then stepped out of her panties. She was naked now, so perfect. His wife.

His stomach tightened. It was so hard to breathe. Noelle was his wife. And it should make no difference to anything, because she wasn't his wife in any real sense. But it did. It suddenly made everything seem different.

So he kissed her again, because that felt good. It made sense.

And when he laid her down on the bed, he tried not to look into her eyes. Tried not to give in to the intense tugging sensation in his chest. But he couldn't manage either.

He looked at her, and he felt like he was drowning. It was like he was completely submerged in Noelle.

He took a condom from the bedside table drawer, an amenity always stocked at this hotel as well, and tore it open quickly, protecting them both. He put his hand on her hip and steadied her as he slid slowly into her.

He had to grit his teeth, hard, to keep from coming then and there, as she enveloped him. Body and soul.

She moved with him, against him, creating a rhythm he couldn't deny. He had no control here. He was lost, and all he could do was let go, let himself get sucked down into the undertow. He didn't have the strength to fight it. And he didn't want to.

He wanted Noelle. Only Noelle.

Always.

His orgasm roared through him, tore at him like a beast before it overwhelmed him completely. It went beyond pleasure, beyond anything he'd ever known. It consumed him. She consumed him.

They lay together, her head on his chest, smooth hands stroking him.

"Did you…sorry, I know you came against the door but did you…"

"Twice," she said.

"I'm usually a bit more considerate but this time…I couldn't think."

"That's okay."

It wasn't though. It was wrong. He needed to keep his head on straight. To have everything organized and to-gether for his acquisition of Grey's. He didn't need to be obsessed with a woman.

More than that, he needed Grey's to matter. He would finally be able to see his father's face as he pulled the rug from under him, and it had to *matter*. Because it was all he had. It was everything he'd been working toward for years.

But right now, it felt like it didn't matter at all.

Noelle rolled over and blinked. It was early in the morning. And Ethan wasn't in bed. It didn't surprise her for some reason. Something had happened last night. And she wasn't sure if it was good or bad. Only that, for a brief moment, Ethan had looked…terrified.

It was all right. It only reflected what she felt.

Terror because Ethan had a part of herself she wasn't sure she could ever get back. Funny though, because he'd also helped her find pieces of herself she hadn't known existed. He had changed her. Or at least helped her figure out some ways to change herself.

It was scary to want someone so much. Scary but amazing. And it made her feel that she wasn't alone.

She got up and reached for the light switch. It illuminated the glossy, opaque glass wall opposite the bed, making it mostly transparent. She could see Ethan's silhouette. Naked. She was getting a view of his shower.

"Luxury hotel indeed," she said.

She watched as his hands slid over his body, her heart rate increasing. There was a certain illicit thrill in watching him like this. Was it what he'd felt watching her play the first time? When she hadn't known he'd watched her? Well, she hadn't been naked but she'd been bare in a way.

If only she could get more than just a sexual thrill from watching him. If only she knew what he was thinking. She felt her nipples tighten, her body aching to have him touch her, not simply to watch him as he touched himself.

She swallowed hard and walked across the room. She was naked, and she wasn't embarrassed. There was no way for her to be embarrassed. Not with Ethan. She was more herself with him than she'd ever been in her life.

She walked into the expansive bathroom and stood in front of the glass shower door. Ethan looked up, water running down his face, his perfect body, the droplets dipping and pooling into the well-defined grooves between his muscles.

"Hi. May I join you?"

He smiled, a purely wicked smile. "Always."

He kissed her, but differently than he had last night. More controlled. She tried to look at him, catch his eye, but she couldn't.

"Ethan?" He looked at her then. For just a moment. And what she saw in his dark eyes made her feel shaky. There was an emptiness there, a distance that didn't seem right.

But then he kissed her again. And his lips were so perfect. And the water was hot and soothing, and Ethan's touch was slick and arousing. So she focused on that.

And she tried to forget the horrible, haunted look in his dark eyes.

CHAPTER TWELVE

"We're going to a small event in one of the high-roller areas tonight. Very exclusive."

Ethan rolled out of bed and Noelle watched each fluid movement with interest. The way his body worked, his muscle structure, his tan skin. It was all so deliciously different from hers. So very sexy. The kind of thing people wrote songs about.

She'd spent the majority of the day exploring it, but it hadn't gotten old. Not even close. The really scary thing was that he was only more enticing now that she knew him so well. Now that she knew just how good things were between them. Now, looking at him made her shiver with the anticipation of pleasure to come.

She was a lost cause.

"We are?"

"Yes. Our debut as a married couple."

For some reason that made her feel...she wasn't sure how it made her feel. Nervous and edgy somehow. She didn't feel ready to go and face people. Not knowing she loved him. Not after everything she'd given him. It felt so personal, and yet she felt as if she was wearing it, as bright and bold as any neon sign on the strip.

"Okay. I don't really have anything to wear."

"That's fine. I saw something I liked down in one of the hotel shops yesterday. I'm having it sent up."

She watched as Ethan dressed, as he covered the body she craved. He still looked good dressed. Though she'd rather picture him naked.

"I can pick my own dress…"

"And buy it too?"

His words cut much deeper than they should. "You know I can't."

"Then you'll wear what I pick out."

"Why are you acting like this?"

He breathed in deeply. "Like what?"

"A jerk."

"I'm just…this is a big thing tonight."

"You never let pressure get to you, Ethan."

"Then I'm allowed a day, aren't I?"

She tried to smile. "Of course. How long until this… thing?"

"Sorry I didn't tell you sooner. I got the call earlier when I went to order lunch for us. But it starts in a couple of hours."

"That's fine. I'm not that high-maintenance."

"No. I know."

The look on his face was strange, that cool distance still present in his eyes. She wanted to erase it. Wanted to bring back the warm man she knew and loved. But he seemed pretty determined to stay gone.

"I suppose I should take a shower. A non-peek-a-boo shower."

He gave her a wicked half smile and for a moment, she could see Ethan again. "I make no guarantees."

"I have to shave my legs."

"You fight dirty. And yet, I don't feel detoured."

"What am I going to do with you?"

His eyes darkened, his expression going flat. "I could ask you the same question."

The dress should have been illegal. He regretted choosing it. It was sexy in an overt way, and at the time, that had been the point. All of this had a point. He was feeling pretty regretful of the whole deal at the moment, at least the part he'd cast Noelle in, but it was too late to back out now.

This was why Noelle was in his life. This was what he'd married her for. He was letting it get muddled in finer feelings and things he had no business dwelling on. He needed to focus on the prize.

Tonight was the night to do just that. He would get what he needed, what he deserved. Tonight was the reason they were in Vegas. And he'd kept it from her. He was a bastard.

"This dress is a bit OTT, don't you think?" she whispered as he keyed in the passcode and pressed the elevator button that would get them to the exclusive high-roller's lounge.

"OTT?" he asked.

"Over the top," she tugged the tight black hem down, trying to get it to cover more of her legs.

"Not in the least. You look every bit the young, hot celebrity. And just like the sort of woman who could entice me into a quickie Vegas wedding."

"Is that the game, then?"

"You know it is." He put his finger on the button again. As if it might make things move faster. As if it might make the whole night move faster. So he could get on with it. So he could get Noelle out of his life and back to normal.

He ignored the sick, tight feeling in his chest.

"Yeah," she said softly. "I know."

And she didn't sound happy. Damn it that he cared. Damn her for making him care.

Why wasn't she what he'd just said? A pretty ornament. A decoration. Why was she so much more? All kinds of extra stuff he didn't need or want from her or anyone else. Why was he letting her split his focus? She was making him doubt what he was about to do, when it had been part of the plan from moment one.

The lift doors opened and he felt his scalp get tight, continuing down through his chest, his stomach. It was like he didn't fit inside himself anymore. He just wanted to climb out of his skin. He would have done, if he could. He didn't know why he didn't feel like himself anymore, why he felt so wrong. And so right. That was the really fearsome thing. He felt more right just standing with Noelle than he ever had before she'd come into his life.

He took her hand in his and led her from the elevator, trying to ignore the slow, spreading sensation of fire that began where their skin touched and made a direct trail to his chest. To his heart.

The hall leading to the high-roller room was long and narrow, the walls black, sleek and glossy, the carpet bright red. Something to make the people who used the casino feel like celebrities.

There were so many things about the place he didn't like. It was more his father's style. Maybe when the ownership of Grey's was transferred to him he would change it. Fix it. But then, this made money. It wasn't really about his taste.

The tacky would probably have to stay. The marks his father had put on the place would stay.

Something he'd have to get used to.

He looked at her again one last time before he opened the door to the private room. She was perfect, blond hair sleek, makeup expertly applied. Her wedding and engagement rings glittered on her well manicured hand.

She was the epitome of a trophy wife.

Thinking of her that way made him feel…it was wrong. They were partners. But tonight she would be playing trophy wife.

"Ready?"

She smiled. "Sure."

He opened the door and revealed an expansive room, all high-gloss and gold-plated. The true mark of nouveau riche. Overdone, overstated.

The room was crowded with couples, men who had women draped over them, fawning. One woman at the blackjack table had two men draped on her arm. A refreshing change, to Ethan's way of thinking. It was the only thing refreshing about the scene.

The rest of it was more of the same. People using other people for money. For sex. The kind of shallow existence his family seemed to aspire to.

That he aspired to. Except what he wanted was different. It *was*.

He scanned the crowd, past the gaming tables. His father was in the corner, a blond probably close to Noelle's age on his arm.

"This way," he said, tugging gently on Noelle's hand, leading her through the crowd.

Damien looked up from his companion, his expression not changing when he saw him. "Ethan. What brings you here?"

Noelle looked at Ethan, her expression filled with confusion. She hadn't known that his father would be here. That the show was for him. But every time Ethan had tried to explain, the words had stuck in his throat. She'd known he wanted revenge. He hadn't told her the part she'd play in it.

"Noelle and I decided to have an impromptu getaway. And wedding." He held her hand up, still clasped in his, and let his father see her rings. "I assume you know who she is. Noelle Birch."

His father's face drained of color, but his expression didn't alter.

He felt Noelle stiffen beside him, but she didn't speak. She didn't seem very present either. He looked at her, just a quick glance, but it was enough for him to see her blue eyes looking glassy, distant.

"Why did you come tonight, Ethan?" Damien asked, his tone implying that he knew perfectly well why. And that he didn't like it.

"To let you know that grandfather is signing Grey's over to me. All I needed was a wife, to prove how stable I was. How much more stable I was than you, and he was more than willing to pass it directly to me."

"You can't have…"

"I have," Ethan said, cutting him off. He turned and put his hand on Noelle's cheek. It was cold. "So now I have your company. I also managed to get one of the Birch women to marry me. Something you never managed to do. Funny how things turn out. Essentially, I have everything that you ever wanted."

As soon as he said the words, he wished he could cut out his own tongue. To treat Noelle like a possession…it wasn't something he'd truly thought through. Or maybe he had. Not simply to hurt his father, but to try and reduce her in some way. Because she was too much inside of him. What she made him feel was too big to handle.

He hadn't fixed anything though. No, far from it. He could feel the fracture between them, the crack in the bond they had built. And it provided him with no relief. Instead, it hurt like the severing of bone from tendon.

"What is it you hope to accomplish with this, Ethan?" Damien asked, pushing away from his date. "Proving the point that you're somehow a man of valor, even while you stand here with your trophy bimbo? You aren't any different. You aren't any better. You're just like me. You always have been, you always will be."

Just like me.

Ethan swallowed hard. "Regardless, I'm the one who walks out of here a winner." A lie. A bitter lie.

He tightened his grip on Noelle's hand and turned away from his father, heading back toward the door. Noelle released her hold on his hand and walked ahead of him, her skin icy pale. Her expression was set, strong, not betraying a hint of emotion. But he could feel it, radiating from her, echoing inside him.

She opened the door and walked out into the hallway. He followed her, his eyes on her, no one else, because she was all that mattered.

He closed the door behind them and followed her into the elevator. Neither of them spoke until the doors closed.

"Why did you do that to me?"

"I didn't do anything to you. It's an act, Noelle." The tension in him exploded, unraveling his control. "All of this is, it has been from day one, and you knew it then, and you know it now. What I said to my father, that was a part of it. I wanted him to face the fact that I did things right and I still came out ahead."

"But you didn't do it right! You lied. You cheated the game."

"Maybe I did, but I'm not the same as him. Someone had to show him. Make him pay."

"And you had to try and be the hero for your mother."

Pain sliced at him and he ignored it, pressed on. "Someone had to be."

"Maybe," she said. "But there was nothing—" She looked up at him, her blue eyes unveiled now, all of her emotion exposed. "—nothing more painful that you could have said. It wouldn't have been any worse if you'd called me your high-priced whore. Because that's what you said I was to you. You reduced me to nothing more than my name. One of your many acquisitions."

Anger boiled in him, at himself, at the damned heavy emotion that was crushing him beneath its weight. It drove him, compelled him to push back. And anger was much easier to embrace than the bigger, scarier feeling that was trying to claw its way into prominence.

"And I'm not the same to you, Noelle? Why did we get into this relationship in the first place? Because I had the power to give you back that wreck you call a home. Because you could use me to get your picture back in the paper, to climb back up onto your diamond pedestal. So don't play the wounded maiden. You got what you wanted."

"Fine. Maybe. But I didn't just parade you through a room and treat you like an object. I have never treated you like an object, or a means to an end. And until tonight, you hadn't treated me like one either."

"Tonight was what *this*, this thing between us, this whole arrangement, was all about. You know that."

"Yes," she said. "We made an agreement in the beginning, and I've held to it. And I knew that being on your arm was a part of that. But now you know me. And you know what my mother did to me, how she used me. I thought that might change something." She choked on the last words.

"It can't."

She looked down, and he looked past her, to where her expression was reflected in the high-gloss obsidian wall.

She looked tired. And sad. And he wanted to hold her. But he was the cause of her suffering, and wanting to be the one to ease it just seemed cruel.

"Well, fine then," she said. "You did it. That's all there is."

The elevator doors opened and neither of them moved for a moment. Noelle felt each beat lacerating her tender heart. She was being beaten, destroyed from the inside out by her own body. Her own emotion.

When they got to the hotel suite he closed the door behind them. The silence was like an entity between them. Real and powerful, hard to break.

"I suppose I'll see about getting my own room."

"You damn well won't," he growled.

He pulled her to him then, his kiss hard, fast, containing all of the rage and frustration and bitter anguish she felt inside herself. It tasted like her own sorrow. Like the ashes and ruin of heartbreak.

And she gave as good as she got. Everything. Because he wasn't allowed to just hurt her and walk away. He wasn't allowed to feel nothing, not when every breath seared her insides. She laced her fingers through his hair and held him to her, hoping to make him feel what she did. To feel all of the pain and desire and frustration.

He wrenched his mouth from hers and trailed hot kisses down her neck, leaving flames in his wake.

"Ethan. Please."

No matter what happened tomorrow. Or in the next hour. She needed him, with her, in her, now.

He pushed her dress up, that stupid dress he'd picked to make her look like a trophy.

"Say my name," she said, working his belt buckle and opening the closure on his slacks. "I need to know that it matters."

"Noelle," he rasped, his voice rough. He slipped his fingers beneath the edge of her panties and tugged them down as he leaned her back onto the bed, her legs still hanging off the edge. He got down on his knees in front of her and shrugged his pants and underwear down his hips, leaving them most of the way on. There wasn't time to take everything off. There wasn't enough time, period. There never would be.

She hooked her leg over his back and pulled him to her. He entered her in one smooth stroke and she locked her legs around his hips, holding him to her, reveling in this moment. In being joined to him. Because nothing made sense. Not how she felt about him, not how he seemed to feel about her. Or didn't feel about her. At least this was honest.

Here and now there was no acting.

She put her hand on Ethan's cheek, and he met her gaze, his dark eyes glittering in the dim light of the room. The tendons on his neck stood out, his breathing harsh, his heartbeat raging. She could feel his pulse echoing beneath her hand, pounding through her.

Every time he entered her, she wanted to take him deeper, to hold him to her longer. She slid her hands down to grip his shoulders, dug her fingernails into his back. He held her too, hands braced on her hips.

The pleasure was blinding, beyond anything she'd ever known. But it was secondary to the connection that was forged, stronger, more permanent, with each breath, with each movement.

He was a part of her. Drawing pieces of her away, bringing more substance back into her. Like sand in the waves.

She fought against her climax, because it meant the end. Because this was the end. She knew it. Knew it in every fiber of being. But it caught her, grabbed her. She reached the peak of pleasure as he found his and they rode the crest together, completely silent except for the harsh notes of their breath.

He withdrew from her body, but stayed on his knees, his arms resting on the bed. Noelle blinked and brushed her hair out of her face with shaking fingers. Every part of her was trembling, inside and out.

She rolled to the side, trying to put distance between them, trying to find a way to escape the pain that was clawing in her chest, pushing out the memory of the pleasure, the closeness they'd just shared.

She looked at Ethan. His face, his gorgeous, precious face. She had never loved anyone like she loved him. Had never needed anyone the way she needed him.

And she knew she couldn't do that to herself. She couldn't keep loving people who didn't love her back. She couldn't keep pouring herself into people who would leave her.

Because as hard as she had fallen when her mother had left, as devastating as it had been to lose her piano teacher, those two constants in her life, if she grew to trust that Ethan would stay…that he would love her when everyone else seemed unable to…she didn't know how she would survive it.

So she had to walk out now. While she had the strength.

She stood up from the bed and walked over to her suitcase. She found a pair of jeans that had remained unpacked and tugged them on beneath her dress.

"Noelle," Ethan said, his voice rough. "Stay with me."

She shook her head.

"Stay," he said again, more desperate this time.

"I can't."

"Why?"

She took a deep breath. "I have an audition next weekend. I haven't practiced at all while we've been here. I need to get back."

"So you can work on your music." It wasn't a question, neither was it an accusation. It was a statement, hollow, empty.

"Yes. You're right. That's why we had this whole relationship. That's the point of it all, you reminded me of that."

She looked at him. He was still on his knees at the foot of the bed and she wanted, more than anything, to drop to her knees in front of him and kiss him. But she didn't. She couldn't.

"I wish you would stay," he said again, his voice muted.

Her chest tightened and she feared her heart would burst from it. "I can't, Ethan. This…this is all fine for a few days," she said, indicating the gaudy room. "But it's not my life. My music is my life. It's what I need."

"Take my plane."

"No, I'll figure something out…"

"Take it. Dammit Noelle, take it." He stood and jerked his pants back up, reaching into his pocket and pulling out his phone. He opened it and punched in a number. "Have the plane fueled and ready to go. Mrs. Grey needs to get back to New York."

"That wasn't necessary," she said.

"It was. You're still my wife. And you will be until the ink is dry on the contract my grandfather sends over. Don't forget that."

No. Of course not. She couldn't forget why they were married. Certainly not for love. At least not on his part.

"I won't." She took her purse from the nightstand and ignored everything else. She didn't want it. She didn't need it. She just needed to get away from Ethan, needed to get out of her skin so she could escape the horrible, sick feeling of grief that was washing through her.

"He was wrong, you know," she said, her voice breaking. "You aren't like him. You're like your mother. You're like I was when we first met. You think…you think you're going to fix something in you by getting revenge, or by getting Grey's Resorts. Just like I thought having my career back would fix something in me. But it won't, Ethan. Not for either of us. It's not about things. It's about people. It's about love. And if you can't figure that out, if you can't find that, then you won't ever be happy. And nothing you have will ever be enough."

Ethan watched Noelle walk out of the room. She closed the door with a finality that rocked him. Still he watched. To see if she would come back.

He was a fool.

He had thought that somehow winning this game with his father, that somehow making Damien pay for what had happened would make him, Ethan…worth something. That he would suddenly be the man he needed to be to make things right. That holding the power, the Grey family legacy, would add some sort of value to him.

The boy who had been ignored by the two people in his life who should have loved him had been working toward this paper, pinning his hopes on it meaning something, for years. Hoping that revenge would prove him to be the better man, that having the family business pass to him would somehow prove him to be smarter, more worthy.

So now he had it. And it hadn't made a damn bit of difference. He wasn't better. He wasn't fixed. His entire life was shattered now, broken into a million unfixable pieces. He had lost Noelle.

He had everything that he'd wanted, that he'd dreamed of. He had billions of dollars and he had notoriety and fame, and yet she had walked away. He had banked on this moment. On somehow triumphing over his father and it mattering in some way, somehow removing the empty, unsatisfied ache inside of him.

Maybe because his own success had never impressed his father. Had never made his mother care.

Anyway, he had done it now, and in the process had increased his own power, his own bank balance. And it had only confirmed what he'd always suspected. Everything he'd feared.

That, as much as he'd wanted to place blame elsewhere, the problem was with him. Revenge had proven to be an empty thing. The acquisition of more hotels, even emptier. Noelle was right. No amount of material possessions could make a difference.

The problem truly was in him. He would never be enough. His love would never be enough.

And he loved Noelle. No matter how much he'd tried to deny it to himself today, no matter how much distance he'd tried to wedge between them with his actions in the high-roller room tonight, he loved her.

Even now that she'd rejected him, walked out the door when he'd all but begged her to stay, he loved her.

And he had let her go. Because when it came right down to it, he was afraid that if he had told her why he wanted her to stay, she still would have said no.

He hadn't been willing to take the chance.

CHAPTER THIRTEEN

Iᴛ wasn't the number she dreamed of seeing on her phone, but it wasn't a bad number to have pop up either.

It was Jacques. Probably calling about last week's audition. She'd all but given up hope on that. But now he was calling, and she was really hoping it was good news. She glanced at the clock, and at the line of people that stretched out the door.

It wasn't a good time for her to take a break, and break-taking was something she had to discuss with her supervisor. Because that was how her new job as barista at the Roasted Tea and Coffee Company worked.

She had a job. And she was learning it, a lot faster than she'd imagined she might. Steaming milk and pulling shots had come pretty naturally to her, and now she could make her own latte. Which was good, since Ethan wasn't around to buy her one. It was a small step on the road to self-sufficiency, but it was a step. One she'd been too scared to take before Ethan had come into her life.

That silly little job inputting data had done so much for her. And Ethan had acted as though she'd done it brilliantly. He'd always looked at her as if she was brilliant. And beautiful. But not the sort of beautiful other people talked about. He said it like he saw something deeper.

Hidden. Something she hadn't seen before he had shown it to her.

Noelle released the catch on the espresso grinder and let a fine dust of beans pour into the porta-filter. She twisted it back onto the machine and hit the button, watching the shot, making sure it took the right amount of time, that it was just the right color. There was a kind of art to this job too, and she found herself really enjoying it. She liked making people smile.

She'd give it all up to play on the stage again, but it was nice to have something else to do.

"Noelle."

Noelle looked at her co-worker, David, who was busy taking orders. "Skinny latte please, a sixteen-ounce, no foam."

"Got it." She put a pitcher of skim milk beneath the steam wand and nearly laughed out loud. Such a contrast from the over-the-top glitz of Las Vegas. Had it really only been two weeks? Two weeks since she'd seen Ethan? Two weeks since she'd touched him?

Then why did her skin still burn? Why did her heart still ache like this? More importantly, would she ever feel right again?

She clenched her teeth to keep from tearing up, something she'd done countless times in the past fourteen days. It was enough to drown in. She wasn't drowning though, she was *doing*. Living.

Because one major difference between having her mother walk out of her life and losing Ethan was that Ethan hadn't torn her down. He'd built her up. Told her she could do anything. He'd left her stronger. Even though he'd also left her broken-hearted.

You left him.

Only because she'd had to. Because someday, in the

not-too-distant future, when he got Grey's in his possession, he would have left. He'd shown her so much. Made her want more than surface fame and recognition. But he didn't seem to want anything more than what was on the surface.

She was starting to wonder if she should have taken the extra time, taken everything he could give. Some days it seemed like her pain couldn't get any worse anyway, so maybe it would have been better to take a bed that had Ethan in it, rather than her big, cold bed back at the manor.

Back at her decrepit old house. But at least it was hers. Ethan had sent those papers already, paid in full. And as far as the public was concerned, they were married. No one was paying close enough attention to realize they hadn't crossed paths in two weeks.

That was another thing she'd done. Gotten her house on the market. Soon she'd be able to move into the city, or just outside of it. Somewhere smaller. More practical.

Someplace where being alone didn't echo so much.

"Sir, I'm afraid you'll have to get in line."

David's distressed tone was answered by a harsh curse spoken in a very familiar Australian accent. She looked up and nearly melted onto the spongy rubber floor.

"Ethan?"

"You work here?" he asked.

He didn't look good. Well, that was a lie—he looked delicious. But he looked tired. Like he hadn't slept for two weeks. Like his whole body hurt him. He looked like she felt.

"Yes, I do. If I didn't they wouldn't let me behind the counter. Employees only."

"Right. Yeah....right."

"Did you have something to say?"

"I've had a lot of things to say, for a long time. But you walked out on me. You left me on my knees."

People, David included, were staring now.

"May I take a break?" she asked, her eyes not leaving Ethan's.

"Please," David said.

She took her apron off and pulled the band from her hair, releasing it around her shoulders, before stepping out from behind the counter. "What?"

"Outside," Ethan said.

"All right. But I don't have long. Jacques just called and if I'm on a break anyway, I should return that."

"Oh. Jacques."

"About the audition."

"Of course." He opened the coffee shop door and held it for her. "How did that go?" he asked when they were out on the sidewalk.

"It was…he said I was a bit too dark. He wanted to hear something brighter from me. But I told him a different day."

"Why?"

"Because I didn't feel bright."

"Any idea why that was?" he asked, his voice rough.

"You know damn well why, Ethan Grey. What are you doing here? Do you need your trophy for something else? Is that it? Did you not twist the knife hard enough into your father?"

He shook his head. "No. I don't need a trophy. I don't want one either. I want you. You were never a thing to me and I…I behaved abominably. And you're right, it was the worst thing I could have done."

"Then why?"

"It was just what you said. You were right. I was look-ing for Grey's to give me some kind of validity. To bring me some sense of satisfaction and purpose that I didn't seem to have without it." He took a sharp breath. "I told my grandfather I don't want the resorts."

"But your father…"

"Can have them. Revenge is empty, Noelle. Vain. It was for myself. All that time I thought that it was for my mother, but it never was. It was for me. I was so desperate to keep blaming my father, to find a way to make it all about him so that I wouldn't acknowledge…I wasn't enough for her. Or for him."

"Ethan…"

"I wasn't as important as her job. I wasn't as important as her marriage. There were a few times when she told me…she wished she had never had a child. It was my fault my father didn't love her. And that day… If I hadn't blamed him…"

"You don't deserve any blame in that, Ethan. You were a child."

"A child whose parents barely looked at him. I… There's something broken in me, Noelle. I know that. But…I still want you. Even though I messed everything up, even though you should say no, and find a man who isn't damaged like this, I want you."

"Then why…" she choked up, her words stalling in her aching throat. "Why didn't you say this before I left?"

"Because I didn't think… I thought if you still didn't want me, even though I was getting more money, more power, then there was nothing I could ever say that would change it."

"You jackass. You thought I would want you if you had more money?" The stunned look on his face would almost have been funny if her chest didn't feel like a hole had been punched in it.

"It was never about you, Noelle. It was about me. Why

wasn't I enough? My mother was so miserable raising me she tried to kill herself. My father has never seen any value in me. Why should you be different? Not because you aren't amazing, but because I just can't seem to earn the love of people in my life. And I've always dealt with it. I've never begged for it. Until you. I'm begging you. And I'll get on my knees again if I have to. I want you to love me."

The image of him, so proud, so strong, ready to crumble at her feet, undid her completely. Two warm tears slid down her cheeks and splashed onto his arm.

"I do love you, Ethan. I have...loved you...for such a long time. But I didn't think you wanted love."

"I didn't. That's a huge part of why I acted the way I did that night in the casino. I was trying to force myself to get back to business. But I couldn't. And in the end I...I don't want to. Love hurts, and I've really gotten a dose of that in the past two weeks. But I've decided it's worth it. Because even though I've never been in so much pain before, I've also never felt so alive as I do because of you. Just because I love you."

"That can't be right." She shook her head.

"You don't think so?"

"No. Because that's how you make me feel. Like I can do anything. You've never tried to hold me back, or tell me I can't. You made me want to try at life again. And I was...scared, so I ran from you, from what you made me feel. But I don't want to run. I want to stay here with you."

"Here?" He looked around them, at the bustling sidewalk.

"Not right here, but you know what I mean."

He dipped his head and kissed her. Warmth flooded her and she felt her heart beat again.

"I want to ask you to marry me," he said.

"Then do it!"

"But I don't want to interfere with your career. With touring."

"Playing again…I want to play again. But it's not who I am. I get that now. I'm so much more than just the piano. Than what the public thinks about me. I'm me. And you helped me figure out what that means. I want to be with you, and if music fits into that, then I'd love to play. But it's not everything to me. It doesn't define me. And that… there's so much freedom in that."

"Then Noelle, will you marry me?"

"I'm married to you already," she said.

"I know, but we'll do it somewhere else, not in Vegas this time."

"I liked our wedding."

"In that case, will you stay married to me? Forever?"

"Yes."

"Thank you, Noelle, for loving me. Just me."

She leaned in and kissed him, her tongue teasing the edge of his lips. "It's not a hard thing to do, Ethan. You're exactly what I need. More than enough for anyone, and perfect for me. Even if I could have all the fame back, all of it and then some, the adoration of millions would never mean as much as having your love."

EPILOGUE

HE loved it when she wore red at the piano. He was certain she did it to tease him. And it always worked. Two years of marriage hadn't seen any of the spark dim in their marriage. If anything, it burned brighter now than ever before.

Ethan watched from the first row of the concert hall as Noelle started to play the grand piano, her fingers tripping lightly over the keys, her slender shoulders working with the rhythm.

The house was packed tonight, filled with people who had come to listen to her music.

Pride surged through him. She'd been playing in theaters along the east coast regularly for a while now, thanks to her resurgence of fame after playing in Jacques' orchestra. And now Noelle played her own music, on her own terms. Not in world-famous music halls as she'd done once, but she never seemed sorry about that. Not even for a moment.

Ethan picked up the program that she'd handed him before the start of the show and opened it. There was a handwritten note inside, done in Noelle's neat style.

Tonight, I'm playing a special song. The one I started in Australia all those years ago. I know how it ends now. Do you? Happily.

Ethan's throat tightened and he looked up at the stage, at the woman he loved. She looked back at him, her eyes shining in the spotlight as she played.

Later he would have to remind her of all the other things he'd taught her. After the show. And after he'd thanked her for all she had shown him.

And for bringing love into his life. Because there was no amount of fame or money that could rival the love they shared. Those things were easily lost, and they both knew it.

But their love was forever.

* * * * *

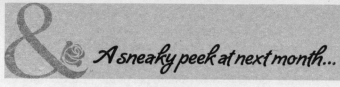

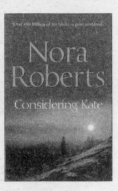

The World of Mills & Boon®

There's a Mills & Boon® series that's perfect for you. We publish ten series and with new titles every month, you never have to wait long for your favourite to come along.

Blaze®

Scorching hot, sexy reads

By Request

Relive the romance with the best of the best

Cherish™

Romance to melt the heart every time

Desire™

Passionate and dramatic love stories

Visit us Online

Browse our books before you buy online at
www.millsandboon.co.uk

M&B/WORL

Have Your Say

You've just finished your book.
So what did you think?

We'd love to hear your thoughts on our
'Have your say' online panel
www.millsandboon.co.uk/haveyoursay

- 🌹 Easy to use
- 🌹 Short questionnaire
- 🌹 Chance to win Mills & Boon® goodies